Live Cargo

by

Pauls Toutonghi

Livingston Press
at
The University of West Alabama

ISBN 1-931982-18-X, library binding
ISBN 1-931982-19-8, trade paper
Library of Congress # 2003108901
This book is printed on paper that meets or exceeds the
Library of Congress's minimal standards for acid-free paper.

Hardcover binding: Heckman Bindery
Cover design: Joe Taylor
Cover photo of Houdini: photograper unknown, taken from
Bob King's HoudiniTribute.com with permission
Text typesetting and layout: Heather Leigh Loper
Proofreading: Derrick Conner, Jessica Meigs,
Daphne Moore, Allan Noble, Margaret Sullivan,
Gina Montarsi

Acknowledgements: I would like to thank *The Boston Review* ("Regeneration" and "In Cities, Together and Apart") and *Glimmer Train* ("Still-Life"), where several of these stories have appeared. Thank you to Jodi Daynard and Linda Swanson-Davies for their invaluable editorial advice. I would also like to thank Bill Henderson and the people at the Pushcart Press. Finally, thanks to the KGB Bar in Manhattan and the Lambs to the Slaughter Reading Series, where "Lives of the Saints" was first read.

Thanks: I'd like to thank my family: Annette, Artis, Danny, Gabrielle, Jarka, John Greene, John Lunsford, Juri and Susan, Mason, Mike, Misha, Morgan Lunsford, Rhonda, Steve, and Tante Renée. Without the support of my parents, Ruta and Joseph Toutonghi, this would not have been possible. *Paldies paldies!* Also, I owe (somewhat alphabetical) thanks to: David Bratton, Adrienne Brodeur, Bob Buckeye, Dave Epstein, Gina Franco, Daniel Gould, Robert J. Greiner Jr., Reesa Grushka, Lee Harrington, Jeremy Kirch, Seth Kolloen, Michael Koch, Josh Michtom, Jay Parini, Kirsten Neuhaus, Tom Pruiksma, Jonathon Reiber, Safety Bear (www.safetybear.com), Tim Spears, Tamara Strauss, Chris Vourlias, Jackson West Wimbledon, Renée Zuckerbrot, Joe Taylor and the fine staff of Livingston Press. A special thanks to Bob Morgan, Dan Schwarz, and Roger Gilbert, my committee at Cornell. Finally, thanks to Sandra Lunsford, on whose idea the end of the story, "A Letter from the Margins of the Year," is based.

Livingston Press is part of
The University of West Alabama, a non-profit organization.
As such, any contributions to the press are tax-deductible.

Table of Contents

For Whitney
By the Love that moves the sun
and the other stars

Live Cargo

Still-Life

Picasso is in his studio in the Bateau-Lavoir, cooking an omelette on the wood stove. There are three brown eggs—two centimes each on the street this morning—and a small iron pan, black, with rust on the handle. The heat from the bulbous stove brings a slash of perspiration to his forehead. The light slants in through the windows that are high-up, that are high near the top of the wall, broad windows, mouths of light, open. The omelette is almost cooked; he inhales the musk of the egg.

It is 1907, a morning in December, and this is what he is wearing: a broad, palm-wide blue tie, a white shirt with a wrinkled collar, a pair of taupe wool pants with wine-stains along their length. There are nearly fifty canvasses in his studio. Most of them face the walls. He has given up on painting; he sketches instead, tracing the lines of his subject with a Spanish-made charcoal pencil.

As he finishes cooking, Picasso retrieves a loaf of bread from the top of one of his smaller paintings. *My shelf,* he thinks, and opens the bag, brushes away a spider with his thick workman's hands, rips off half the remaining loaf. Standing over the stove, he eats the omelette and thinks of the night just past, a long night, and the crooked smile of the whore with whom he's slept. He thinks of the way she half-smiled when he left, how she kissed him softly on the left side of his face.

He looks down at his eggs. *Baby chickens,* he thinks. *Infants.*

He dips the bread in the yellow soup and remembers her citrine odor, the lingering scent of the sweat and stubble along the insides of her thighs. Not unlike the smell of the eggs, actually, he thinks, and then he is startled by a knock at the door.

Picasso pads slowly into the hallway. It is Fernande, his wife. She has opened the door and let herself in. She is walking towards him. *Damn,* he thinks. *Damn.* He sees that she is crying.

—I'm sorry, he begins. I'm sorry. I was here. All night, I was here, I swear to you.

Fernande shakes her head. She wipes her nose with the back of her wrist.

—Never mind that. You have to come quickly. Wiegels has hung himself. I couldn't cut down his body.

IN THE STORY my grandfather tells me, he is a conscript in the Turkish army.

It is 1915, and he is serving just east of Suvla Bay, a few kilometers from Anzac Cove and the fighting. It is August, and the sea kicks the linen scent of its salt into the air each day, a scent that is mixed with something else, with the sweet reek of decay and raw blood.

My grandfather's task is the assembly of customized weapons. The factory is a makeshift, dusty hangar, an enormous, single-story warehouse built from plaster and stone.

Each day, he spends his time filling forty-centimeter cartridges with high explosives, metal scraps, and a percussion cap. He then grafts the shells onto the end of two-meter long sticks, sticks that are the thickness of a man's arm. The soldiers hurl these from one trench to the next, often during the middle of the night, when the explosion, he is told, looks like a sunrise.

Each morning, the colonel in charge of the munitions plant comes into the barracks and chooses a man to polish his shoes. These are luxurious, expensive leather shoes. They have a beautiful grain, they are thin as a sheep's stomach, supple. While the soldier polishes them in the colonel's quarters, the colonel eats his breakfast and sings. One day it is a love song, one day a holy song. He has a terrible voice, and his mouth is often full of boiled eggs.

—What did you think of my singing? I wanted to be a muezzin, you know.

—It was very good, sir.

—It was? Would you care for an egg?

—No thank you, sir.

—Are you certain? I just bought them last night on the street. They're fresh.

When you are done polishing the shoes, my grandfather says, the colonel gives you three Egyptian cigarettes. They are cheap, sure, but the smell is unmistakable, and they have a certain prestige. You smoke them on your breaks, in front of the other men, while you perform. Sweating in the August heat, you sing the morning's songs in a steamy contralto, your voice cracking and crackling like oil in a pan.

PERSPECTIVE. A FACE, slightly deviant, arranged at such an angle. A relationship of light, a luminous body of paint, Ripolin colors, synthetic wood or canvas. Picasso and Fernande, and they are running through the narrow alleys to Wiegels' studio. It is a wet cold morning, with ice in the gaps between the cobblestones, with an occasional lowskimming gull coming in off the

Seine. Picasso has not slept. He has been wearing the same clothes for days, and the sweat has begun to itch, to dry and stiffen and itch. Fernande is sobbing as she runs, and he can scarcely understand her.

—We were drinking. And hashish. And ether. And then opium.

The cold air is stinging her face.

—He went home. He smiled and he bowed at the door. He actually bowed as he left. I went to see him this morning. I hoped you'd been there, you know. I hoped I'd find you on the couch.

—He did it right there? In his flat?

—Near the window.

They slow as they approach the building, and Picasso looks and sees the figure on the second floor, sees it immediately, indistinct behind the glass. He has been working, for many months, on his new method of painting the whores, on the Bordello, *le Bordel,* and now he visualizes only lines, only broken geometries and disconnected stories. The top of Wiegels' ragged boots, Picasso sees, even as he goes through the door, are still moving to the left and to the right, south and south-southwest, tracing through the air like a gentle pendulum.

IN THE STORY my grandfather tells me, he is a volunteer in the French army.

It is 1915, and he is serving near Verdun, in the low, green-stained hills. He has a new velvet hat, a freshly-made képi, and it is causing him problems—chafing, pinching, giving him a headache.

Les barbelés, he leans forward and tells me, the barbed-wire—

it was like a mouth. It sucked you in, like a mouth. I was tangled once, for a moment—that's where I lost my first hat, *ou j'ai perdu mon premiere chapeau.* And such a beautiful hat, that one. A fine, nearly perfect stitching, with only one or two misplaced threads. Wool so soft you couldn't believe it came from sheep. I was glad I made it out of the wire, sure. Men never lasted in the wire—anyone could tell you that. But when I crawled back into the trench and realized that I had lost my képi, I wept like a little child. A hat meant a lot to you, you know, in the war.

In the war, he says and then he laughs softly, a sound dry as yeast. I was an artist, you know, a sketch painter. That didn't mean I wasn't in the fighting. I was there with all of them—with Bonnard, Moreau, Zadkine. And they were drunkards, you know, even in the trenches. I was lucky to leave the war with a liver, the way they made me drink. Zadkine especially. He was the worst. You look at his sketches—his India Ink with pale blue and his simple yellow, his little cubes—and you have no idea. How could you? A tremor here, a certain translucence there? No. You just can't trace these things.

One time, I was near some fighting, near a place where the trenches had started to break down. I saw, from a distance, what I thought were some corpses in a ditch. I made my way through the field, slowly through the field, and I looked into the mouth of the hole. You were drawn to these things, you know, you couldn't help it. It was a crater from a shell, the kind that usually had bodies in it. This was no exception—two dead men, one of them missing an arm. But also—and at this I fell backwards, at this I stumbled backwards and lost my hat in the brine—there was Zadkine, sitting in the fetid water, soaked, and drinking whiskey from a bottle.

He didn't see me at first, so I waited and I watched. I was speechless, you know. He was drinking the whiskey and then he was passing the bottle to the dead men. He had pried open their mouths and was pouring the stuff down their throats. Finally, after two or three circuits, he saw my hat floating nearby. He raised his eyebrows and looked up at me and grinned, he showed me his toothy, charismatic, drunkard's grin.

—A cup! He started shouting. Why, Victor, you've brought us a cup! How nice of you. Une tasse! Une demitasse. Une képitasse. *Tres bien*, Victor. Well done.

Picasso is sickened. He looks at the ground, at the walls, at the unfinished paintings that line the path to the doorway. Fernande is in the other room, in the kitchen, slumped against the wall. He cannot do what he must, and so he sits at the breakfast table near the window, a few meters away from the dangling body. There are fresh-cut flowers here—tulips, bright red and incongruous in the December day—and Picasso sees Wiegels' pipe, stuffed thick with fresh tobacco. He waits a moment, drums his fingers on the tabletop. And then he picks up the pipe, brings it to his lips. He takes the matchbox from his left pocket. He starts the flame on the grout between the cold tiles of the floor.

—What are you doing? Fernande has heard the rush of the igniting match, but she cannot bring herself to look around the edge of the doorway. Her voice is trembling. Have you done it yet? We need to walk to the police.

Picasso coughs a little at the unfamiliar tobacco, then exhales a mouthful of juniper-colored smoke. He looks up at the body for the first time, and notes the stains around the eyes, the terrible angle of the neck. The trail of some mucus—perhaps it is vomit—lingers along the lines of the chin.

—I'm waiting, he says to Fernande. Wiegels left his pipe. I want to smoke his pipe.

IN THE STORY my grandfather tells me, he is a novitiate in a seminary on the Italian coast, a few miles to the south of Amalfi. It is 1915.

His brothers are in the war, of course, but since he is so young—only fifteen, just like the year—he has not yet joined the fighting. The priests swish through the hallways in their laundered soutanes, pale and aloof, hands clasped stoically behind their backs, moving as if they aren't tethered to the ground. In the mornings he prays with them; in the afternoons he pieces through the Gospels, reading, memorizing, constructing a faith and an identity; in the evenings he walks into the hills nearby and sings the mass, sings it to the sharp slip of the rust-colored land as it feeds into the Mediterranean. *Introibo ad altare Dei*, he intones, and spreads his arms as if the whole of the sea is his altar.

Then, one humid Tuesday afternoon—sometime after two o'clock but before half-of-five—he falls suddenly and passionately in love.

This is how it happens, my grandfather says, and opens his hands in the air, a gentle supplication.

I am walking to town for news of the fighting and three dozen eggs, walking along the road that I always take, wearing what I always wear, my best shirt and collar. It is rare that I am called upon to go into the village, since I speak so little of the language and am unsure of the customs. Near the last farm before the town wall, I see her: she is reading a book on the steps of her home, wearing a rose-colored hat, drinking something from a wine-colored glass. It is these colors that get me, more than anything else, these two perfectly matched colors. As I pass by her, she looks up. She sees that I am staring. She smiles at me, and notices that I wear the uniform of the would-be Jesuit.

—What are you reading? I ask.

—St. Augustine, she says. *The Confessions.*

Composition à la *tête de mort,* Picasso calls it, the painting of Wiegels' studio with the body near the window, done in scissored cubist forms, in minimal color.

It is late one night, only months later, and he brings it home to show to Fernande. It is a great labor, carrying this painting through the streets, this painting that is wide as his arms are wide—all heavy canvas and wire and frame. He is not a large man—this is difficult for him, a tremendous exertion. Picasso is coughing and sweating heavily when he comes sideways up the stairs. He clatters his burden onto the wooden floor of the apartment. He sees her immediately, lying on the ground, drinking red wine from a clear glass, reading a book beneath the arc of three candles.

—Fernande. Look. I brought it back. To show you. I've finished it.

She doesn't look up.

—Fernande?

—Is this the one we've been talking about?

Picasso is looking at the thing, looking at the way the paint rises from and falls back to the surface. He is looking at the places where the texture of the canvas can be seen, where the paint thins away and the fabric asserts itself. His voice is soft.

—Yes. Yes, it is. I finished it today.

Fernande stands and walks to the kitchen. She doesn't turn around.

—I don't want to see it then. Take it back.

At first he doesn't understand. He is lost in the memory of creating it, of moving his brush against the background, of choosing one shade from another, one movement from another. He is amazed at how it contains time, right there in its movements, in its angles and its subtractions. He is thinking of this and then he is beginning to understand her voice, he is turning to Fernande and he is angry.

—But it's so far. And cold. It's cold tonight, near freezing.

—I don't want to see it. Why don't you understand?

—But Fernande—

—You are so stupid, Pablo, so thick. This is my flat too, you know. I don't want it here.

She has her back turned, and her two hands are pressed against the wooden counter. Her black hair falls like a drape, cutting off the light that would rise, luminous, from her skin. He looks at her, thinks of his weary muscles, of the weather, of the walk. Then he remembers something else. He sighs. He bends and lifts the painting from the floor.

—Save some wine for me, would you?

He leaves quietly, bumps twice into the wall as he descends the staircase.

The Lives of the Saints

Telepathy, Julia figured, was out of the question.

But this man was so beautiful—reading a book on his lunch hour, drinking hot tea from a porcelain mug—this man was an improvisational masterpiece. A luxury of smooth black hair swept along the line of his jaw. Turning the pages—and he seemed actually to be *reading*—he occasionally paused and looked through the café windows with his blue eyes, crinkling his forehead into little rows of thought. And his biceps. Julia could see them, now, pressing through the knit of his cotton shirt. She imagined the pale knots of them, hovering above her body in bed. She imagined the musky scent of his aftershave.

Even though she'd given up on her book, Julia maintained the image, shifting the pages at the proper intervals. This was necessary, of course. Everyone here wanted to *look* as if they were reading. Gansevoort Street was the new literary hub of Manhattan, or so it seemed, at least between the hours of noon and one p.m. This particular café was called Silo, and it was on the margins of the Meatpacking District. Its owners had decided to decorate only the ceiling. The walls were concrete and steel, but anyone who leaned backward and looked up would see a series of video monitors projecting images of dismembered display-window mannequins. The installation was called, *Hostile Makeover: A Guide to Modern Beauty,* and someone had assured Julia that it was quite charming. This had saved her the neck strain.

But her man, her subject—how could she get his attention? She could knock over her coffee, or drop something on the floor, or cough. But then she would seem inelegant or clumsy or sick. And first impressions invariably laid the groundwork for sexual attraction. And that's what she was looking for—she was being completely honest with herself, here—sex with a magazine-quality man. Sure, it was her lunch break, it was probably his lunch break, the whole of the city was out having lunch. But you had to do your research if you wanted in the game. If he wore a wedding band, if he was uninterested, or gay, or unable to speak English—this was how she had to find out. If he was unbearably dull or stupid—well, these were short-term obstacles that could be overcome.

Julia McKinley was about to be downsized. She was an online-content editor, a tech-Marine, first in and first out, *semper fidelis novum economicum*. She had graduated from Columbia on a Saturday, had interviewed on the following Monday, and had secured the job by the end of the week. She'd elbowed in on the ground floor—a little company with powerful, niche-marketed ideas. Life had been so gracious, so fortuitous, so simple. At twenty million in options, her boss was a genius. He smoked cigars in the hallways, drank Mickey's at board meetings, was always quoting Shakespeare. He kept a basset hound in his office that he insisted was a stockholder. Then things started to slump. At ten million, he was a troubled dot-com mogul. This snared him the magazine covers, the human-interest features, the interview on MSNBC. He was highly respected, Julia came to understand, within the community. At no million, though, he became a crook and a fugitive from the law. One Friday, she saw him going into an abandoned warehouse near Brooklyn College that was famous for its S&M parties. He was on the cocaine circuit in Williamsburg. Then he left the country. Word on the street said he was in Bali, working on an organic farm. The CFO had taken control of things now, and he'd made public his plans to fire everyone but himself. The stock was at twelve cents. It was about to be kicked off the index. Within weeks she would be on unemployment.

Julia aired these tech-sector troubles in late-night phone conversations with her Latvian grandmother. Marija Kukulis—the matron of the family—lived in a small, pink ranch home just north of Chicago. She was close to ninety years old. When Julia called her, the phone rang ten, eleven, twelve times and then, quite suddenly, a thickly accented voice would assert itself in the darkness. Marija's last name—as she would often remind her granddaughter—meant 'loaf of bread.'

—Julia, *mana bucina,* my little kiss, do you know what my name means?

—*Ja, oma*, it means loaf of bread.

—Is right. And do you know who I married?

—*Ja, oma*, you married a baker.

—Is right. And what I did in morning every day thirty-nine years?

—You worked in the bakery, *oma*.

—Soft in the middle, hard on the outside. Just like bread. You'll make it through, *mana bucina,* you'll make it through.

NEARLY ONE O'CLOCK. He was liable to leave at any moment.

He would blend his way down the stairs and into the warehouses and the warm March day. And then he would be lost—tragically gone forever—a pleasant but wistful memory, a half-remembered moment of beauty. Preparing herself for the walk to his table, Julia looked casually at her reflection in the back of a spoon. She gasped. Dear God—was she that fat? And why was she upside-down? On the edge of panic—and then high school physics came rushing back to her. Concave mirrors. Only beyond the focal point, Julia remembered, did your reflection seem smaller and thinner. And you were always upside-down, no matter how far away you went. Maybe it was unwise, Julia thought, to look for a metaphor in everything.

And she'd been reading Plato's *Republic*.

It was embarrassing, really—reading this kind of a book in a public place. You never knew who'd drop in. And if they saw you, and they knew you, they would invariably saunter over to your table. And they would ask, then, *What are you reading?* And if you said, Oh, just some Greek philosopher, they would laugh and say, No, *really*. And that was what she wanted to avoid. So she'd bought a remaindered old Proust at the used bookstore and switched the dust jackets. Proust was much more suitable, really, and she even practiced the pronunciation of the French title, letting it ring through her sinuses like a rough bout of allergies.

But her man, her object—he had stopped reading and was only staring, floating through some contemplation of the windows. They were truly massive windows—the kind you saw in Gilded Age public high schools built by grants from Rockefeller—and the metal panes had rusted from ceiling to floor. The rust gave the light a well-framed, granulate quality, a grainy yellow tinge, as it came through the glass in segments, in divisions, in streams. Julia's man looked sadly at the light. As if it were all part, she thought, of some beautiful but slightly disappointing drama. And there they were—his blue eyes—and they were indeed quite nice. Such a ghostly color—dramatic even from the other side of the room. But then she tended to overplay these things. Her coffee was getting cold.

Julia stood, adjusted her blouse, walked a few steps. She paused, brought her hand to her hair, walked a few more steps. When she was just in his peripheral vision, he looked up, smiled slightly, and his teeth were perfect. She smiled at him, too, doing her best to look calm. They're just like dogs, she thought. They know when you're nervous. She cleared her throat. But don't worry. Just say hello. All shall be well—all manner of thing shall be well—if we keep to the upward way and pursue justice with the help of wisdom. Right? Is my lipstick crooked?

IN HER DREAMS, Julia is an ancient Greek philosopher, but one of the lesser figures—the RC Cola of the Hellenic intellectual scene. On this occasion she's helping Socrates build himself a house—nice real estate, good view of the sea, orchards of olive trees, no hemlock. They're working on the kitchen which, owing to the time period, is sparse on appliances. The air is scented with salt and the bacterial perfume of the dune grass. There are a few seagulls here and there. Noisy, they hover in the air like kites. Socrates is laying the bricks for the foundation of the stove. Julia is mixing the grout, adding sand to the substance that will anchor the kitchen tiles.

—How are these proportions, Socrates?

—Do they seem right to you?

Julia looks out through the windows. This is just the annoying kind of thing that he says all the time. She taps her fingers against the surface of the putty-like mixture.

—Why can't you just answer me, Socrates?

—Where are the answers but in ourselves?

She sighs. The hills really are beautiful, though. They fall off—a rocky soft-shimmering green—into the sea. The waves crackle and purl against the shore. The Aegean is a cake. A frosted, diminishing, white-daubed cake. And the only good thing about Greek philosophers, Julia decides, is the toga. She sighs again. Socrates looks at her then—he's noticed this continual sighing—and he releases the brick he's been holding in his left hand. It hovers, inches above its final destination.

—What's wrong, Julia? Is it the men?

—The men? The men? Of course it's the men. How could it not be the men? Don't you know? Haven't you figured it out? I broke up with Bill three weeks ago. I'm torn up about it. Can't you tell? I made a huge mistake.

—You idiot. No, wait. I'm sorry. Don't you think that you're an idiot?

—Of course I do. But that's not the point.

And here Julia starts crying, her head on the puffy folds of Socrates' flowing, white robes. They really are soft, she thinks, softer than you would expect. They have a certain plushness about them. A certain padded nature that is tremendously pleasing. Socrates strokes her hair with his thick, inelegant fingers.

—Well, shouldn't you call him, then?

—Oh, shut up, Socrates. You're no help at all. And why the hell are we building a kitchen anyway?

This is when she wakes up.

Admittedly this was, for her, a time of profound life-crisis.

At least this is what she told her therapist, who seemed interested only in the most sordid, sexual details of her life. *I am in a time of profound life-crisis, Arthur*, she said, for that was his name—Arthur Krackle—despite its obvious absurdity. But the main absurdity was this: Since Philip Roth and Woody Allen, therapy had lost its value to her. When she was a freshman, sure, she could sit in the office at psychological services and answer the routine questions about eating habits and depression. But now she was paying for these sessions, and whenever she looked over at her analyst all she could imagine was *What's New, Pussycat,* and there was Peter O'Toole in his shiny black wig, grinning a lascivious grin.

—It's the men. And I keep dreaming about philosophers.

—I see.

—Not sexually, or anything.

—No sexual dreams involving men?

—No. No sexual dreams involving philosophers. Well, Socrates is really the only one.

—You're having sexual dreams involving Socrates?

She sighed again and again. No, Arthur, no. You have it wrong again. You're supposed to tell me that all the characters in my dreams are reflections of myself. And that the auto-erotic fantasy is traditionally interpreted as a symbol of post-modern disintegration. Then—and only then—you should recommend an expensive prescription drug made by a major pharmaceutical company in which you own stock. Julia rubbed her nose. To sigh, she had to inhale, and the odor of Arthur Krackle's office was aggressively musty. When was the last time he'd dusted? And it was unpleasantly noisy in here. The single window was thick, but not thick enough, and the sounds that filtered in from the street were somehow more terrible because they were muted. He needed a miniature fountain or a stereo playing Debussy.

The light and the heat were both tepid.

Julia realized that she was surrounded. That they were roughly fifty percent of the population. No amount of therapy could erase this gloomy fact. She emerged from her apartment each morning and there they were. Daily, she bought her bagel and her coffee from one of them—a tubby one, admittedly, who operated a silver concessions cart that wasn't much bigger than his body. She elbowed through their sweat and slithered through their offensive eyes on the Subway. The 1/9 swept her from Grand Army Plaza to Christopher Street, spit her out into a workplace that was teeming with their bacteria. She toiled beside them all day. They were graceless and bulging and enjoyed violent sports. They sought to desecrate and insinuate, to confiscate and legislate, to delegate and inseminate—all at the same time, if possible. And then, if she was lucky, she slept with one on a Friday or a Saturday night.

Arthur Krackle cleared his sinuses powerfully.

—Well. Our time is up, Julia. See you in two weeks?

AND YET THIS MAN, here at Silo—her current subject, object, and verb—he looked up at her as she approached. Julia didn't know what to say, but did know that she suddenly had an expectant audience. She raised her eyebrows.

—Can I touch your arms?

There was a moment of silence between them.

Then he smiled.

—You know, that's the strangest line I've ever heard. I'm Ronald.

She paused. Again with the ridiculous names.

—Just your biceps, Ron. They're beautiful. My name is

Pandora.

—Really?

—No. Actually it's Julia. But I'm serious about the biceps.

Ronald extended his arms to her, a mute offering. She rested her hands on them and they felt just as she had anticipated: slightly warm, lined with an industry of arteries and veins. But what was she supposed to do now? Having a plan would have helped, she realized, with this part of the process.

Maybe she could look into his eyes, see if they carried any traces of his character? It was ridiculous, sure, but still it was pleasing to think that this could reveal something—the look in the eyes, searching and deep, just like a Victorian novel. *I'll see the far reaches of your soul,* Julia thought. *I'll know if you like pad Thai.* She pursed her lips, tilted her head to the side.

—Can I have your phone number, too?

Ronald didn't hesitate.

—No.

—No?

—Of course not. I'm engaged. And you're totally crazy. Or at least you *seem* totally crazy. Maybe that's what you're going for.

Julia nodded. This was understandable. It was all so understandable. She leaned forward precipitously, giving him the option of looking down the front of her blouse.

—Thanks anyway, she said. See you later.

She walked down the stairs and through the door.

In her dreams, Julia loiters outside of a male strip club, trying to gather the nerve to go in. The billing is tacky—big black letters on a fluorescent-lit background:

Socra-tease
All-Male Review
Are we the best
LIVE NUDE ENTERTAINMENT?

A group of women comes around the corner, laughing and visibly drunk. Julia bluffs her way into the crowd, passing through the door with her head down. The bouncer seizes her shoulder with a meaty fist.

—I.D. please.

Julia laughs.

—Forget it. It's my dream. Get lost.

The club is even smokier than she anticipates. There is a thick layer of carpet—surprisingly spongy beneath her feet—and pipes of bubbling, neon-tinted water. Nearly-naked waiters scurry everywhere—they are a bounty of musculature and gently-lit flesh. Some of them wear bunny ears. Julia finds the bar, orders a Coke. She straddles the barstool and sips at her drink, looking dubiously at the spectacle before her. There are both women and men in the audience. The men are seated mostly near the front. What are the parameters, she wonders, of a male lap dance?

Then the music starts, low and pounding, more of a pulse than a beat. A husky female voice comes over the P.A. It is much too loud, and tinged with feedback.

—Are you ready to get Greek tonight? Are you ready?

There is a mixture of jeering and applause.

—Tonight, for one night only, fresh from the clubs of Athens, together in Manhattan for the first and finest time, ladies *and* gentlemen, let's give it up for the hottest bad things to ever hold a Symposium: It's Socra-*Tease* and his All . . . Male . . . Review!

And here they come, one after another, wearing only their togas, entering in sequence to the rhythm. There's Phaedrus and Pausanias, Aristophanes and Eryximachus and Agathon. And then—last in line, plump and stately and wearing nothing at all—the man himself, the philosopher/stripper/superstar. He begins to dance, throwing his hips to the left and to the right. It looks like a rhumba.

Now didn't Socrates always say, Julia tries to remember, that the philosopher has erotic value in his ideas alone? Then why is his body greased—she wonders—in a way that erotically accentuates the curves of his potbelly?

Such are the dreams of Julia McKinley.

She walked out onto the street, leaving the café and squinting at the newly bright light. It was a great day, one of the warmest of the young year, and there was a damp eloquence about the city. Warehouses rose from the streets in a way that implied dew—that suggested what could have been if, say, Manhattan Island were still a grassy, Dutch-owned homestead. Here and there a window was open. The air off the piers was only a little sour. Quite suddenly—with the air moving in and filling the broadest part of her lungs—Julia realized that she was not going back to work. And it wasn't complicated, either. It would just end, right now, with this turn on Waverly. She stood at the corner and blinked. She wasn't going back. The street seemed vast, an intriguing possibility of unemployment.

Last night, Julia's grandmother had read to her from the *Lives of the Saints*. She did this frequently, depending on the severity of her granddaughter's crisis, and Julia regarded it as a kind of additional therapy, free of charge, in the style of the forgotten past.

—Here we go, Julia. March twenty-eight: My favorite. Saint Guntramnus.

—Guntramnus?

—King of Burgundy, it say, 561 to 592. A bad man.

—And he's still a saint?

—Oh, sure. He divorced one wife, it say, and killed some doctors.

—Doctors? What for?

—It doesn't say, you know. But see—even he became a saint. He killed some doctors. You never know, *mana bucina,* anything can happen.

Julia didn't point out that most of these saints were martyrs, and that she wasn't planning a heroic death any time soon. Nor was she debating the execution of any medical professionals. But why worry her grandmother?

And besides, Julia took a certain pleasure in this unfolding of the calendar. She kept a little sketchbook and jotted down notes. There were familiar characters, like Saint Nathalan, January 19th, who locked his arm to his leg in penance for his sins, and then threw the key into the River Elbe. Or Saint Julian the Hospitaller, February 12th, who mistakenly slew his parents. Or Bishop William Tempier, March 26th, who fought a lifelong crusade against simony. Exactly what simony was, Julia was unsure. But looking it up in the dictionary, she felt, would ruin at least some of the pleasure.

These phone conversations were the remains of a life that Julia had surrendered when she'd come to New York at eighteen. *The Lives of the Saints*—sure, they were crazy stories, stories of people who were rabid for martyrdom, eager to slip off their skin in exchange for something eternal. But maybe this was what she was lacking: A certain rabies of the spirit, a devotion to something other than the analysis of herself, an abandonment of control.

Julia walked from Waverly onto Bank Street and then—rounding the corner, looking up at the chapped sides of the warehouses, maroon against the light blue sky—she tripped. Falling to the pavement, Julia flung out her hand and encountered something soft and yielding and thick. She hit this object and then rolled and looked back and saw what it was: an elderly Asian woman lying prone, wrapped in a thick pink winter coat, clutching a paper bag of groceries. The woman's mouth was open. There were small yellow squash spilled in a halo to the left of her body.

First Julia looked around, searched for anyone else to help her. There was no one. The street was strangely empty—no pedestrians, no loading trucks, no taxis. She looked helplessly at the corpse on the pavement. The woman had been on her way home from the market, it seemed. Her purse had fallen a few feet from her body. The tip of her wallet was visible, and a pack of gum, too. Only one of the sticks—Julia noticed as she lay there—had been consumed. Was it a heart attack? She was definitely dead. Julia felt the side of her neck. It was slightly cool to the touch.

—911, this is Sherry. What's your emergency?

—I'm calling to report a body.

—What is your location, ma'am?

She had walked across the street to the nearest phone booth. Her fingers had felt ghostly as she dialed the numbers. Then she'd crossed back over, sat next to the cooling body. The woman's face was gentle, frozen into an expression of surprise that seemed remarkably peaceful, given the circumstances. *Should I close the eyes?* Julia thought. Wasn't that what you did at a time like this?

—Mind if I have a piece of gum?

It was cinnamon flavor, a brand Julia had never heard of.

Somewhere, far away within the catacombs of the city, a police siren began to wail. The flavor started on her tongue and spread outward, saturating her mouth with its sweet sting. Julia inhaled. She slipped the pack of gum into her pocket. She reached out and took the old woman's hand in hers, feeling its bones and its smooth skin. Even the air of the city, it seemed, was tinged with the traces of cinnamon.

Stalin's Favorite Pig

Comrade Balodis was busy being overproductive.

He sat at his desk, chewing on a blade of grass. It was a rich, flavorful blade of grass, one of the best of the young spring, redolent of the winter snows, tinged with the slightest expectation of summer. Balodis chewed and chewed, turning the pulpy fiber over in his mouth. He made a notation on his legal pad: *Grass: good. Sample again tomorrow.*

For the last ten minutes, Balodis had been disturbed by a frantic pounding—a hammering, really—on the dusty glass of his office door. There had also been shouting, and because of it, his tasting of the grass had almost been disturbed. It was unforgivably rude, he considered, bothering a man in the midst of his morning's duties.

Balodis sighed and looked at the door. He was ready to listen. He heard the voice of his supervisor, shrill and gargling behind the glass.

—In the name of Lenin, Nikolai, let me in! I demand you let me in right now!

Iurii Sokov was a demanding man. As the vice-commissar of Division 12.4 of SOGOR, the Bureau of Livestock Handling and Feeding, he seemed to sweat paperwork. It appeared from his pores at an alarming rate, trickling down steadily to all of his assistants.

—You're welcome to come in, Comrade Sokov. I am awaiting your every instruction.

—And if the door is locked?

—Only the door can answer the riddle of its own nature, Comrade.

Balodis chuckled softly to himself as he fumbled with his key ring. The best thing about the Union, he considered, was the opportunity it provided to end a sentence with the word *comrade*. Who could resist? This was the real reason, Balodis considered, why the Soviets would triumph and the Americans would fail. In the United States, the bureaucrats had no hope of irony. They labored in tedious obscurity, hoping only for retirement, or possibly new uniforms. With this one little phrase, this simple comrade, SOGOR became an enchanting place to work, each day full of sarcasm and wit. Or something close to this.

—Comrade Sokov. What can I do for you?

—You can learn to answer when I knock, first of all. Sokov spat on the wooden floor. Drunk at your desk again, Nikolai?

—Not at all, Iurii. I've only had a little vodka. With breakfast, you know.

Iurii Sokov shook his head. He cleared his throat and set his arms across his chest, puffing himself out to an even larger size. The workers at SOGOR, of course, ranged from portly to obese. They feasted on the finest smoked sturgeon, the palest gray caviar, the richest duck liver imported by boat from Paris. This was the saying: In the Soviet Union after the Second World War, if you wanted danger, you joined the KGB. If you wanted dinner, however, you became a bureaucrat.

—I should fire you, Nikolai.

Sokov paused and waved his hands in a small circle in the air. He rested his chin on his chest, the rolls of blubber gathering and swelling. He continued:

—I should fire you, but everyone must work. At least now you can be useful. Stalin's favorite pig is loose again.

LARGE ANTIPERSONNEL BLAST MINES, SOVIET PMN SERIES.

11.2 centimeters in diameter, loaded with 150 grams of RDX-TNT. The shock waves, they'll tell you, can explode outward at 6,800 meters per second. Victims stepping on these large antipersonnel mines, they'll say, invariably suffer a traumatic amputation. Quite often the lower part of the leg is blown off. A piece of the tibia may protrude from the stump, and the remaining muscles are pushed upward, giving the leg the appearance of a head of cauliflower. A head of cauliflower? You'll say. They'll nod. Often, they'll continue, the opposite leg is also badly damaged—frequently with gaping wounds and open fractures. Penetrating injuries of the abdomen or chest are fairly common, too.

IT ANNOUNCED THE END of what had been such a wonderful morning, full of rest and careful contemplation. Stalin's favorite pig was a foul-mannered Georgian sow, a big creature with a voracious appetite and a love of escape. She was a porcine Houdini, and could free herself from any pen, sty, or barn—slipping through windows and walls and barbed-wire fences. And then, Balodis would have to find the beast, and it would take him all day, sometimes more than one day, blundering through the mud and weeds and sparse scrub forests.

Balodis didn't remember how he had come to be called *Pig-Man*, or *Protector of the Pig*, or *Stalin's Beloved Swineherd*. He couldn't recall the first time he'd rescued it, or why, or under what circumstances. All he knew is that he would invariably get the summons—once or twice a month, in the form of Sokov, his supervisor, pounding on the dusty glass of his door. Then he would take a private car to Melensky Prospect, chewing, the entire time, on his nails.

Located forty minutes from downtown Moscow, Melensky Prospect was a sprawling collective farm, with fields of beets and cabbage and carrots and wheat, with livestock pens and a buzzing apiary, with a productive and fragrant apple orchard. Its buildings formed an imposing complex: six greenhouses, a pentagon-shaped research dome, opulent living quarters like few others in the Union. This was the home to Stalin's chief agricultural scientist, Trofim Lysenko. It was also where Stalin came when he craved the labor of a farmer. To his comrades at Melensky Prospect, Stalin was both icon and compatriot. He was vicious and intimate and, for some peculiar reason, he often worked with the pigs.

Stalin would wade into the sty in his army-issue wingtips, performing all of the standard veterinary concerns—the inoculations, the examinations of hooves and teeth. Smiling from beneath his broom moustache, he would whisper lyrics from old Georgian lovesongs to the sows, patting their fertile bellies. After a visit from the Chancellor one spring—a reliable source informed *Izvestia*—each mother gave birth to a litter of seventy.

Often, he and Lysenko would drink late into the night, grafting plants together, injecting chemicals into rabbits and mice. Then, when the darkness was deepest and most complete, Stalin would summon a secretary and walk out to visit the sty. *Some of these pigs,* he would say, *are Heroes of the Soviet Union. This one,* and he would point unsteadily into the herd, *and that one, and that one. They deserve the Red Banner of Labor.* Dutifully, the secretary would record the number of decorations, and sketch—as quickly as possible—little caricatures of the chosen pigs. Within days, a few of the animals would be decorated, the medals of honor hung proudly around their fatty, pink necks.

Stalin's favorite pig was a smallish pink animal, with a distinctive red mark between his eyes. *The mark of genius*, Stalin said, pointing to his own face, even though he had no birthmark. The secretary agreed, of course, quivering as he spoke.

—Yes, comrade Stalin, I agree. It is, of course, a genius. Both yourself, and this pig. Geniuses.

Stalin nodded vaguely from beneath his moustache. *Note to self,* he thought. *Insubordination. Have secretary arrested and tortured.*

Deportations.

In the 1930s, the Trans-Siberian railroad was double-tracked—one set for livestock and industrial freight, one set for passenger cars. By the middle of the decade, the government had developed the longest nonarticulated locomotive in the world for the cross-country trip, the 4-14-4, whose engine alone contained seventeen tons of pig iron and steel. The 4-14-4, however, often destroyed the tracks when it came into curves, bursting wildly through the gauge and into the frost-bound tundra.

Prisoners from the Gulags, of course, repaired the railroads. Often, inmates even built them, working their way into their prison terms, laying track for the very trains that carried them to internment. Camp labor constructed the Baikal-Amur line, the Trans-Siberian line, the Moscow-Volga Canal. Wearing striped cotton uniforms and battling all possible variations of inclement weather, political prisoners starved and died while they drove the spikes that bridged the east and the west of the Soviet Union.

THE PIG WAS FAMOUS.

It was like that with everything he loved—musicians, steel workers, sports, food. One day in the spring of 1950, with feelings for America still lukewarm, *Izvestia* had published this photo of Stalin:

Comrade Stalin Loves Strange American Apple

The caption read.

Just Arrived By Air From United States.

It added.

For weeks Moscow was in turmoil. Everyone searched for the pineapples, scouring the shops closest to the Kremlin, the ones owned by the government's Requisition Committees, the ones that were stocked with the finest in black market goods. At first, the shopkeepers were amazed. They had Jack Daniels American whiskey, sure, or Lucky Strike American cigarettes, but they'd been given almost no food—no beef or bread, no chicken or sugar or eggs. And yet here were the three-star generals, the politicians, the mafia—all of the men who had caused the shortages in the first place—and they were madly enquiring after something they'd never even seen, after some sort of spiky bourgeois fruit.

Soon, the grocers grew tired of the inquiries. They hung butcher-paper in their windows, long strips of it that read: 'No Pineapples.' One enterprising young store manager proudly posted a banner that said: *Pineapples Here! Fresh This Morning! Limited Supply! Hurry!* When the customers arrived, of course, they found that he'd just sold the last one, but that he had a fine selection of Jack Daniels American whiskey, or Lucky Strike American cigarettes. After two days of this, however, an angry mob confronted him at closing. They seized him and dragged him into an alley, where they stole his money and shot him in the head. The papers praised the crime as a revolutionary act on behalf of the proletariat.

So when it became known that Stalin had a particular favorite among the pigs at Melensky, and that this pig had a birthmark—a bright red stain between its eyes—the other farmers began to single it out, to give it better food and health care. They were constantly grooming it—cleaning its back and massaging its ears. They spoiled it. No matter what the pig did, no matter how many times it escaped, Balodis, the Pig-Man, was always summoned. He would track it down, feed it, and restore it to its sty.

Of course, there were jealousies. A plot was uncovered to poison the pig, and seven conspirators were deported to Vorkuta. The editorial staff of *Izvestia* joined them. Stalin, it seemed, had never even seen a pineapple—the entire photo was an elaborate practical joke, an image that had been cropped and altered in the newspaper darkrooms. The government, however, was notorious for its lack of humor. Balodis himself was the one to sign the orders of deportation. SOGOR handled all requisition forms for livestock cars and locomotives, and so the task of signing away lives often fell to one of its deputies. The job was easy, Balodis often reflected, as if you were just writing on a page with a pen.

HOG CHOLERA.

Hog Cholera is a highly infectious disease of swine. It is characterized by an inflammation of the lymphatic glands, kidney, intestines, lungs and skin. Its lesions are hemorrhagic in character, with the bodily organs showing deep red spots or blotches. Confusion results from lesions in the brain.

In 1903, De Schweinitz and Dorset produced typical hog cholera by injecting hogs with cholera-blood filtrates. The cholera hog, they demonstrated, sheds the virus through its bodily excretions. The symptoms may differ widely in the various outbreaks of the disease. Disorientation may occur. Recovery is rare.

THE CAR LEFT THE KREMLIN just before lunch, a long black sedan with an uneager minister in the back. From his perch atop the stiff leather seats, Balodis watched the boulevards of the city open and unfold. There was Uspenski Sobor and its three golden domes, there was Kafelnikov Square with its legion of skinny pigeons, and there was the quick transition from city to farmland, as the car sped towards Melensky Prospect, its driver mute and staring mechanically at the road.

And Melensky was oddly empty. The driver left as quickly as he could—he hopped back into the Lada and sped out through the farm's main gates. There was simply no one around—a rarity for a Monday morning on a farm as large as this one.

Balodis inhaled the smooth, grass-scented musk of the rural air. It was good to leave Moscow, even under these circumstances. He would retire someday, he resolved, to the collective farm, and he would work only half-days, and he would drink his pension in vodka. He ambled towards the living compound, listening to the absence of voices, the long krull of the crickets, the slip of the wind through the alder and the birch. It was raining, only slightly raining, and Balodis paused to collect himself. He ran his hand over his face, cupped water in his palm and rubbed it into his eyes. *I have to concentrate on the pig*, he thought, and then, just then, he heard a cheer of sorts, distant and dim, coming from another part of the farm.

The complex was mostly dirt roads, six of them, arranged in a grid. It was well-planned, precise, and modern—rectangular concrete barracks clustered around the central dining area. Balodis walked only a few minutes before he found the commotion. The farmers—all of the farmers, it seemed, speaking their various languages and milling tumultuously about—were gathered at a barbed-wire fence near the farm's eastern perimeter.

Balodis came up a small hill and pushed his way towards the front of the crowd. This was one of the minefields that ringed Melensky—the vestigial reminders of the war that, even after a few years, had been officially discarded into memory. Balodis elbowed his way to the left and to the right, but still he couldn't see. Only brief glimpses of the field—an overgrown tangle of weeds and ragged little trees—swam into focus, partial and light green.

—Balodis said, What's happening?

—It's the pig, someone replied in accented Russian. Stalin's favorite pig. It's sitting in the middle of the minefield.

Three pounds of fish per month—a meager ration—and the political prisoners would consume its totality. They dried the cod's skin and made a sinewy jerky. They dried the cod's bones and made a thin soup. They ate its eyes like jellied fruit. And it was almost impossible to escape from the camps. Out in the tundra, a man wouldn't survive overnight. The mosquitoes would strip him of his blood. Invariably, they would stick to a sleeping man's face and start feeding—in the morning, he wouldn't be able to open his eyes.

The pig was indeed sitting in the middle of the mines, propped on its back legs, chewing on something invisible, possibly its own mouth.

—It's sick, one of the farmers said.

—It's gone crazy, another one said.

To Balodis—who by now had made it to the fence and could gaze out into the field—the pig looked essentially the same, mischievious as always, focused at the center of attention. From time to time, it moved its weight to the left or the right, and at this movement, the farmers would yell with anticipation—a chorus of anticipation—hoping that they were about to see the thing explode, to burst and scatter its innards in a ring of pink and red.

Balodis wondered why, of all fields, the pig would pick this one. Mined as a training course for the Fourth Army Fusiliers and Minesweepers, Moscow Battalion, it was clearly marked, for anyone who could read the loping Cyrillic figures: *Deadly Mines! Keep Away!* The pig, of course, could not read Cyrillic. Or maybe it could. Maybe it had obtained a map, and maybe it had a steel plate in its belly, metallic and insulating, like armor. It would kill its keepers, one by one, taking pleasure in the massacre. Whatever the case—even if it was sick or dying or homicidal—Balodis had to get it back. He was the Pig-Man. But whether to go into the minefield, or to try and coax the thing out, he couldn't decide.

The choice seemed outwardly simple. Get a carrot, or a cabbage, or a tub of swill, and stay where it was safe, on the good side of the fence. But Stalin complicated everything. This sow was such a beloved animal. Stalin loved her absolutely, as it was said he loved no other human, and whether or not this was true, Balodis could not confirm. But he did know that anyone who harmed her, directly or indirectly, would easily forfeit his own life.

He paused for a moment, stooped in thought, leaning against the wire. And then, there it was, a boy—six or seven years old—running as quickly as he could for the field, ducking through a gap in the fence and sprinting through the tall grass.

—I'll save Stalin's pig! He was shouting. I'll save it! I'll be a hero!

And his mother was running behind him—ten meters behind—and she was shouting his name and trying to stop him, and she too, made it to the fence, but she got stuck in the wire, she couldn't make it through, and her boy was screaming and running towards the pig and the farmers were cheering in ten languages and then suddenly, as if this moment had been planned all along, the boy reached the safety of the pig and tackled it dramatically to the ground, throwing his full weight into the animal and tumbling through the dirt. There was no explosion.

It was now clear that the boy would be a hero. He would seize the pig by its collar and lead it back along the route he'd just run—miraculously, miraculously and by the grace of Lenin, alone—and both he and the pig would be safe. Who was he? What was his name? Was it Peter? Or was his mother screaming Pavil? No one could tell—she was hysterical and bleeding from deep abdominal gouges. Her son was the new Pig-Man. He was the Pig-Boy! *Someone free the Pig-Boy's mother from the fence*—a farmer called out in Russian—*her dress is snagged and she's weeping hysterically.*

Did any of them notice the old Pig-Man? If they did, Balodis quickly reflected, it was only with a cursory sideways glance. The pig was safe, sure, but Balodis had been proven completely expendable. His job now belonged to an eight-year old. He would take the bus back to his offices, where he would sit down to work and work for twenty years. Or maybe he would be deported. *Failure to fulfill the duties of command.* Balodis imagined the orders he had signed, imagined the cold, clattering livestock cars, winding their slow way towards Siberia. With Stalin, you just never knew.

In one motion he was climbing up the fence, raising himself above the other members of the crowd. He pressed his head through the barbed wire, felt its sharp tips gouge into the flesh of his cheeks.

—Boy! He called. Boy! Listen to me! Don't go back the way you came. Walk straight to the fence. Leave the pig there. Walk to me! It's your only hope for safety.

There was a murmur in the crowd. What was he saying? Wasn't that Balodis, the old Pig-Man, the one who was supposed to save the pig when it got into trouble? Where had he been all morning? Drinking at his desk in his plush Moscow office? Everyone knew what could happen if the pig was lost. Wholesale execution, deportation, torture. With Stalin, you just never knew.

—Don't listen to him! Someone shouted into the shocked silence. Go back the way you came! And take her with you.

But Balodis was waving his arms, and he seemed so concerned, so earnest, so authoritative. As if hypnotized, the boy began to move towards the fence. One step, two steps, three steps, and he was making it across the field. Closer and closer to Balodis, and the farmers were retreating from the fence, falling back in anticipation of the explosion, but it looked like the boy would make it, he was only a few steps away, he was so close, and then there was a soft click, and the bulk of the gathered crowd dove for cover, and the explosion sounded like a car door closing, and there was a shower of maroon, and a quick moan, and Balodis was blown off the fence backwards, and the boy was lying on his side, legless and unconscious, and then the boy's mother was screaming again, and she had worked her way free of the fence, had torn off most of her dress, and she was running towards her son's body and she, too, stepped on a mine, stepped on two in immediate succession, and they ripped her body simply apart, like eager teeth through the flesh of a plum.

"We are still way behind the capitalist countries in the beet crop," complains Molotov, and his complaint could be extended to every branch of agriculture—textile as well as grain growing, and especially to stockbreeding. The proper rotation of crops, the selection of seeds, fertilization, the tractors, combines, and blooded stock farms—all these are preparing a truly gigantic revolution in socialized agriculture.

From: Leon Trotsky's *Revolution Betrayed: What Is the Soviet Union and Where Is It Going?* Printed in exile: 1939

The pig died three days later, of cholera. Balodis attended to its final moments, nursing it with a bottle, desperately trying to hydrate its failing body. A few hours after it died, there was a knock on the door of the livestock pen. Balodis—who had been drinking his vodka steadily for several hours—struggled to his feet. Or was he really standing? Was he imagining this from the floor, where he was lying, nearly unconscious, the alcohol burning and heavy in his stomach.

He saw the shadow first. Then he saw the face, the most distinctive, well-known face in the world, dramatic with its sweep of moustache. It was the face of his brother, his father, his lover, his confidant. It was the face of the revolution, as it stood, today, circa 1953, in the outbuildings of Melensky Prospect. Stalin looked at him.

—You did all you could.

His voice was surprisingly gentle Balodis thought.

—Thank you, Comrade Stalin.

Balodis rubbed at the back of his neck, suddenly sober. He'd done all he could, it was true. But what else was there to do? This was a revolution, this was a feast of love, a feast of industry, a feast of the future. And Balodis was here, as close to its center as a man could get, and it was sad—exhilarating but sad.

—Will you help me, Comrade Stalin, in burying the body.

Stalin nodded. *Of course he would help.* The pig would be heavy to lift. The two of them stooped, together, and began to raise the beast.

A Map of the Air

If you believe me, this is how it happens:

Commuter flight, O'Hare to LaGuardia, seven in the morning on October 10th, 1999. The sun is a hazy smudge of orange off the left wing. There are precisely thirty people on board. Six are in first class, twenty are in coach, two are stewards, two are pilots. The duration of the flight is one hundred and thirty-three minutes, and in those minutes the passengers consume eleven bagels, nine ounces of cream cheese, fourteen oranges, two grapefruit, six measures of vodka, and a whiskey sour. Most are asleep.

As a moment in time, this flight is entirely unremarkable and unredeemed, a moment like any other in the stubbled, episodic wash of daily life. There is not a live-birth, or a heart attack that turns out—thankfully for all involved—to be only angina pectoris. There is no food poisoning, rude behavior, or unusual turbulence. The bypass-duct on the *Pratt and Whitney PW-100* does not become clogged, resulting in a catastrophic loss of power to the turbo-prop, a failure which causes the plane to plunge, without warning, thirty-two thousand miles down into the sea. There are no ambiguous sexual episodes. One of the passengers in first class does request an extra pillow, a pillow with a goose-down core if at all possible, but otherwise, nothing happens.

Charlie Fisk is seated at the back of the plane, where he most enjoys the ride, where it can, once in a great while, become almost interestingly rough. He has made this trip several hundred times in the past ten years, and the airplane is, to him, a second skin, a weariness through which he moves without thought or effort.

On this day, as on any other, he is working his way through the morning's crossword. His pen skids over the newsprint, leaving hesitant marks here and there, small traces of thought, of pause. Thirty-six across: Four letters. Yugoslav ruler and member of the Jackson Five. Charlie's pen ticks across the surface. *Tito,* he writes, a small weight of pride moving up through his shoulders and his neck.

At first, Charlie mistakes the sobs for some mechanical function, for some sort of mechanism engaging secretly in the concealed workings of the plane. Then, tilting his head at an angle, ceasing the movements of his hand, he hears it: the grain of the voice, the ragged breath of someone crying. Immobilized, pinned to his seat, Charlie Fisk watches the lavatory door, listens to the woman weep.

When she emerges it has been almost ten minutes, ten minutes of uninterrupted sobbing, of half-muffled grief in the airplane restroom. Charlie's unsure when she managed to walk past his seat, to push her way hurriedly through the door, to slide the lock into place and brace herself against the confining walls. As far as he knows, she sprang from the substance of the lavatory itself, from the warm ooze of the liquid hand soap, from the coarse paper towels that are stacked, implacable and white, in their little horizontal compartment.

She is beautiful, though, and this word hangs in his mind as he looks briefly at her form, at the angular jut of the bones of her face as she walks past him. *Beautiful.* Her eyes, he sees, are a pale blue, and her skin is slightly yellowed with sickness, the color of raw linen. She is wearing a bright red dress. The hem of it sways along the line of her calves as she walks up the aisle, as she disappears through the curtains that partition first class from coach.

Without any hesitation, he unbuckles his seatbelt and hustles into the unoccupied restroom. Smiling a little, bringing his tongue out and over the tips of his little pointy teeth, Charlie luxuriates in the oddly illicit feeling of using the bathroom immediately after this beautiful woman. Her heat and her perfume have stayed behind her—part lavender, part lingering shit—and the seat of the toilet is still warm, he notices, still slightly damp. Disturbed by what he is doing even as he does it, Charlie squats and inhales the musky air near the mouth of the bowl. The scent is tumultuous in his senses—the odor of fecal decay and of partial sanitation.

That's when he sees it:

It is snagged in the door to the trash bin—a wet and crumpled piece of paper.

Charlie takes it in his hand and unfolds its creases. He is gentle. He is careful not to tear the nearly-translucent membrane. The woman has obviously run the paper perfunctorily under the faucet. Water has blurred the ink, dulled the thick black strokes into long, looping swirls of gray.

Dear Mitchell, it says.

And then, immediately underneath: *Dearest Mitchell. Mitchell, my love. Dear Mitch.*

CHARLIE IS FASCINATED. Still kneeling, he reprises, again and again, how the woman stepped through the folding door and into the cabin of the plane. He imagines her movements—pausing, briefly pausing—as her hand negotiates the intricacies of the opening. How she looks down to be sure of her footing. How her skirt clings faintly to her body as she walks away, all redness and movement and sorrowful sex.

The note, he thinks, and looks down at his hands, his hands which are about to finish the woman's work, to let the note slip its quiet way into the oblivion of the trash.

He has already read it, of course. He hunches there near the bowl of the toilet and touches his fingertips to the runny ink, imagines that he is lingering over the skin of the woman, imagines her own hand holding the pen, holding it mawkishly because she is crying, holding it like a child would hold a marker, unsure.

> *I don't know how to say this because I love you so much Mitch. I'm so confused. I love you and I guess I'll just say this I'm pregnant. And it's so hard but I've decided*

And that's where it stops.

Charlie taps the paper, scratches the stubbled lump of his chin.

I've decided to keep the child? To abort the fetus? To leave you, Mitch, and elope with the baby's true father—your cousin Freddie, the plumber, who inherited the family home in Hackensack, just across the bridge? We make love there, Mitch, every Monday, Wednesday, and Friday, right after work, in his waterbed near the palladium window with the majestic view of the sun setting over Home Depot. We make love and drink Jack Daniels and bathe our naked, tumultuous bodies in the sweet reek of sex. We bathe them, Mitch, and now, for the sake of our son, we want to build a new life together, build it with our reeking bodies, build it in Hackensack without you.

Charlie looks up and into his reflection in the lavatory mirror. For a moment, he sees himself as he is: an aging, rumpled tissue of perversion, a hopeless actuary with a list of petty addictions and an unglamorous few years ahead of him. He is squatting next to a toilet in an airplane restroom, mongering through the life of a complete stranger. He smiles.

This flight has, he realizes, become almost somewhat interesting.

When Charlie stands his knees give off an arthritic pop, a rustle in the joints, the smallest whisper of death. He moves his own hand to open the folding door.

ARE YOU STILL with me? If you are, then stretch out, relax, loosen those muscles. No reason to do this all in one sitting. I've got a lot left, believe me, and we have as long as you want. I know I'm not going anywhere, at least.

The thing to remember is this:

Commercial air travel is, in many ways, a profound act of faith.

This space that Charlie Fisk traverses—this cold, color-poor vastness—is one entirely foreign to the human body. Placed in empty air, the individual falls. However, when he is lucky—and when he is wrapped in the armor of momentum and torque and steel—then the individual maps a path from one point to the next, from city to city, country to country, continent to continent. He has the weight of helium. He is all blur, a frightening mathematical equation.

Long ago, when Charlie first began these audits, he was filled with a sense of companionship, of closeness with his fellow travelers, with the nameless men and women who accompanied him on his journeys. But this hasn't been the case in so many years. Since he turned thirty-five, really, he has been accompanied only by a sense of duty, of boredom, of vague and centerless depression.

Now, however, this has changed.

He returns to his seat and sits down. He buckles his safety harness. His mind will not be still. It returns, like a circuit to the source of its fault, again and again to the idea of the woman. She must be in first-class, he realizes, sitting next to her lover, next to Mitch, who has no idea what is happening within her body. Of everyone—and not just everyone on the plane, but everyone alive, everyone anywhere in this world—Charlie shares a hidden knowledge with this woman. For Charlie Fisk, this knowledge is a profound and wonderful thing. Though it divides—though it stubbornly separates him from others—it also fills, it fills him with an indistinct love, a sensation that he somehow remembers from college.

But what is her name?

And what will he do—what will she mean to him—once they deplane?

IT'S AN INJECTION of saline solution that triggers the uterine contractions. The doctor's assistant sluices the pulpy matter into a plastic sack, which she then seals and deposits into a long, plastic-topped box. In this box there are three other bags of amniotic fluid and blood. When the time comes to close, the doctor's assistant places all four samples on the disposal cart.

At midnight the janitor comes through.

She is wearing mismatched cotton socks (one black, one gray) and smoking a cigarette as she walks the quiet halls. It is so still in the clinic at night—unusual even for a public building in the darkness. The janitor remembers other jobs she has worked since coming to America five years earlier, an immigrant in the first waves out of the crumbling Soviet Union. Cleaning a public high school, a county courthouse, cleaning the rooms at the Ramada just up the Deegan, a few miles from the highway. She brings the smoke into her lungs and for some reason, she's thinking about herself. She laughs, because this is a rarity.

This job at the Bowery Clinic: it's the most *precise* she's had, the most precisely silent, the job where the silence has counted most perfectly for what it is.

Listen, now, because this is important.

Imagine yourself moving down the hall behind her, shaky and sudden, lit only by the auxiliary fluorescents. Imagine her hand, imagine the warts on the back of her hairy knuckles, as she begins to push the cart down the hall, a moveable feast. The left wheel sticks a little, rattles a little, and then, as she comes through the double swinging doors, it begins to squeak.

OR MAYBE NOT.

Perhaps instead you must imagine forceps—enormous forceps—about the size of a tube of celery. The obstetrician puts them between her legs, slides them slightly inside her dilated vagina. *He's going to dent the skull*, she thinks, popping through the surface of her narcosis. The coagulants and painkillers have removed her head from her shoulders, substituted a clean span of gauze. *He'll pop it like a grape.* Then the redskirted woman is thinking about her hipbone, which is round and solid beneath her skin, and a liquid across it, a warmth of trickling blood. She has forgotten the plane and the note and Charlie Fisk and even, in the confusion, her lover, her Mitch. There is a feeling inside of her as if she is lined with quicksilver. She glimmers and shines with the heat, and then the head is there, she can feel the head. And she imagines the eyes, human eyes, emerging out of her, opening for the first time, seeing only the stained skin of her stubbled thigh.

It must smell terrible, she thinks.

RECOGNITION AND REVERSAL: Charlie sees her as soon as they clear the walkway to the terminal, sees her walking with Mitch, holding his hand as they head towards baggage claim. He is fat, this Mitch, and Charlie immediately resents him. Resents him for the waddling way he walks, with his belly in front, comfortably filling the fabric of what is, Charlie sees as he gets closer, a very nice suit.

Baggage claim.

A citrine glint rises from the metal borders of the rotating carousel.

Charlie imagines these three scenes, in order:

1) He executes it perfectly. A tap on the shoulder, a bow, a theatrical flourish of the hand.

—Hello, madam. I am Charles Fisk. I would like to speak

with you in private.

There is a murr in the belly of the machine as the baggage begins to slide down the chute. Mitch recoils, his face rising into a sneer, thinking, *Who's this loser?* But the woman smiles. The nameless, red-skirted woman smiles, and she says:

—Mitch, you wait here and look for our bags, all right?

Mitch mouths something in impotent confusion. Charlie and the red-skirted woman walk a small distance away. He looks at her eyes. They are somewhere between blue and red and purple, and he smiles, and he says:

—What's your name?

And she tosses her hair—it is a snake of hair, eloquent and venomous—and she says:

—Mathilda.

He laughs, Charlie does, because this is wonderful. And he explains to her that he found her note, that he wants to tell her that he knows, that he *understands*, that he loves her beautiful, swelling stomach and that he will support her, no matter what she decides.

They are talking now—in this hallucination of Charlie's—but somehow what they are doing is not really talking. There is language, sure, or at least there are sounds that resemble language—sounds that, heard as they are, become more of a sonic collage, a roughly audible constellation. It is more of a video clip of talking, actually, and then there's a band in the corner, and they're playing on a little silvery platform, and they're fronted by Peter Gabriel, and somehow, somehow, there's Mitch on drums. From this point onwards—Charlie Fisk realizes—his life will be one endless video clip, minus the credits, and Mitch will always be playing drums in the corner, pudgy and regular, fully downloadable.

2) He executes it perfectly. A tap on the shoulder, a bow, a theatrical flourish of the hand.

—Hello, madam. I am Charles Fisk. I would like to speak with you in private.

There is a murr in the belly of the machine as the baggage begins to slide down the chute. Mitch recoils, his face rising into a sneer, thinking, *Who's this loser?* The red-skirted woman is anxious, clearly confused by Charlie's intrusion. She is threatened and worried and unsure.

—Who the hell are you? Mitch says, and Charlie suddenly understands that it has all gone terribly wrong. He scrambles to defend himself.

—A friend. I'm an old friend. From school.

—From school? He your friend, honey?

—I never seen him, Mitch. Never seen him before in my life.

—Which school was it?

—Which school?

—That you and Matty went to?

—Oh, well, it was Garfield High, just down the street, on the Q10.

—I've never gone there, Mitch. You know that. I went to school in Jersey.

—Look. She don't know you, buddy. You heard her. She went to school in Jersey. Now get lost.

Charlie backs away, his secret knowledge burning against the sac of his lungs and in the center of his chest. He knows that he is crying, and he also knows, sadly, that he has lost her, lost his beloved Matty forever.

3) Different place, different time. A week later, a month. No, three months, almost—let's say a night in January, just after the turn of the year. Charlie is passing the clinic on Bowery, having just left the small holding company where he's been conducting, since the day after Christmas, a full audit.

As he passes by the building, Charlie happens to glance to his left and there—large and metallic in the alley that is no more than ten feet wide—there is the hazardous waste disposal unit. A dumpster. And the gate—the barrier that bridges the gap in the cyclone fence—the gate is slightly ajar.

Charlie pauses. He is seized by a powerful, inexplicable impulse—one that he can't defeat or even struggle against. He looks up and down the block. No one. Quickly, more quickly than he has moved in years, he slips into the alley. And then, with one, complicated motion of his hands, Charlie uncovers the dumpster and leaps over its edge. The top clatters shut above him. He is inside. Darkness. Why is he here? He has no idea at all. And the stench of old blood, somehow familiar as his own scent in his own bed in the morning, rises up from the floor and nearly makes him sick.

THESE THINGS ARE ALL, of course, imagined.

In the actual world, in LaGuardia, on the 10th of October,

1999, nothing like this happens. Instead, Charlie follows the couple to baggage claim, waits beside them as they also wait for their luggage. They are talking, just a little, discussing what they saw on television this morning—some commercial, as far as Charlie can tell, for a department store. The crowd of people waiting for their possessions to appear is fairly quiet. One man talks on a cellphone. To Charlie, the morning seems remarkably soft—almost gentle—a light-infused, morning-softened crowd of people, waiting obediently for their things so that they can go.

He drifts off. There is a murr in the belly of the machine as the baggage begins to slide down the chute. He almost doesn't notice when Mitch moves towards the carousel, when he bends forward and takes the two duffle bags off the belt.

Charlie watches the red-skirted woman offer to take one of the bags.

Mitch refuses.

The woman kisses Mitch's cheek and shakes her head, smiling, smiling as she turns away from Charlie Fisk and, without even saying goodbye, walks through the mechanized terminal doors.

Regeneration

If the devil wore cologne, the workers muttered, hacking into a stubborn flank, a thighbone.

Each of the seven dead elephants weighed close to five tons. This number, Hulbert understood, was an approximation. Whether it was slightly more or slightly less, though, he reflected as he dug at the dirt on either side of a dirty yellow tusk, didn't matter all that much. By now—gracelessly splayed at the back of its pen in the Berlin Zoo, its tusks sunk in the dirt, half of its carcass stripped of skin and sectioned into ten-pound packages of bone—the elephant did not care much about its self-image. *Too fat? Too thin? Too concave, too convex? And my trunk—too serpentine and scaly?* The elephant could rest; the elephant could cease from worrying.

—Maria, no. No. I'm too tired.

—You're all dust, Hully. I'm all dust. We need a bath.

—Maria, I—

—What? We'll lick each other clean.

—Maria—

—My name? An epiphany. My name. Lights, an angel, a repetition.

THE ASPARAGUS CAN dig? This morning's supervisor had asked this, his forehead drawn into a jumble of creases and folds. Then he'd sighed and extended a shovel. Among the prisoners of war—the large men with bony forearms and shaved heads—Hulbert was immensely foreign. But he did work for a single ration coupon. For flour, for bread, for soap. He was economical.

IF THE DEVIL wore cologne, the workers muttered, hacking into a stubborn flank, a thighbone.

HULBERT HECHT LEANED against the bone, the exposed ivory that was stained with rivulets of blood and the truculent, yellowish mud. Tiredness gathered in his muscles, in the arms that had been digging for hours, in the burning backs of his heels and his knees. Last night, lying on the tattered mattress that he shared with Maria, he had looked down at his legs in wonder. His knees were swollen as cabbages, almost luminous in the damp light of the cellar.

—BOY!

Hulbert flinched mid-motion. This meant him.

AND SHE HAD kissed his mouth and his hairless, thin-ribbed chest. And now, standing in the swirling dust of the cold November day, wearing his only sweater—the sweater he wore everyday to ramble around Berlin, to search for work among the clean-up crews—he had found a job repairing the wreckage of the zoo. And it stank, even though most of the bodies of the dead animals had been removed. Only the elephants remained—seven of them—and they had to be ponderously dissected, cut into manageable chunks and carted off to the landfill.

—*SPARGEL!* ASPARAGUS! ARE you listening to me?

—Yes, sir.

—How is the tusk coming, Asparagus?

—Almost free of the ground, sir.

—Well, hurry up, hurry up. When you dig it clear I want you to saw it off. And then, I have a delivery for you to make. You think you can lift this tusk?

Hulbert looked at the thing, still solid in the jawbone of the beast. The prisoner closest to him laughed, briefly, a sound that skittered into nothing as soon as it began, a muffled exclamation. The Unteroffizier spun around.

THE ELEPHANT COULD rest. The asparagus can dig. Maria delivered notes to the wives of the executed men. The war widows. Soldiers, politicians, bureaucrats. Sometimes she whistled as she walked down the street; once she tripped over a dictionary. It was stained and torn, coverless, in the gutter. Had someone tried to burn it? What an odd book, she thought, lifting the heavy, wet paper. Mud on the first few pages. She picked a word at random. *Kompott*, she said aloud. Stewed fruit.

At the doorway to the first woman's house she paused. Didn't she remember this place from some other time?

—What? Are you laughing? Are you, *taube*?

Pigeon.

—No, sir. I . . . I . . . cough.

—Coughing?

He kicked the man hard, in the abdomen. Already weak from hunger, the prisoner curled over onto his side, his lips opening and closing, trying desperately to tongue the air into his chest.

Ruth Wagner gave him bread and lemon jam, dirty yellow, the color of dried moss. *Your beautiful mother,* Ruth said, *gave me lemon jam when I was sick. In my tea.* The light was almost texture, marbled in the panels of the dust. Hulbert coughed into the towel that Ruth held to his face, just short of his lips, a dishtowel. Crane-light, light like the neck of a crane, and she touched his light brown hair with two hesitant fingertips.

—They'll pick each other clean. Like animals. Like vultures.

She thought for a moment, brushing the bruises on his chest.

—No, Hully. We did the right thing. We were beautiful today.

EVEN THIS SECTION of it was heavy. He felt it burrow into the plane of his shoulder. What address did he need? The dust was abrasive against his skin, his eyes. *Unter den Linden.* First left. South on Wilhelmstrasse. And then, a wound in the ground, great as some reptilian mouth, and there, in the half-dim, a pair of boots with the legs still in them. No body, just legs. *But these are such good boots*, he thought, and sighed, continued walking. *What a shame to waste such good boots.* And the city was a sewer. It stank of shit and decay and corrupted flesh. He continued walking. Water pipes cut from a rubbled span of gravel, a citrine column of water cut through the grimy noon fog. If the devil wore the air, Hulbert thought, his body would be such sweet cologne.

YESTERDAY, HULBERT HAD seen the Unteroffizier execute a man in the wildebeest pen, shoot him in the head for eating raw meat off a carcass. Afterwards, Hulbert had heard the commander talking to the other officers; the man had to be shot, he'd said, because he had become sub-human. *Just imagine*—and here the Unteroffizier had raised his hands in the air and paused, looked quickly to the left and to the right, a conductor initiating the orchestra's responsive swell—*just imagine kneeling over the dead body, and chewing at the bloody, fatty flesh.* Zoofleisch. *Just imagine. It was, quite clearly, the sickness of his race, coming through under adversity. But still . . . and we work so hard to educate them.*

Barbaric Slavs.

MARIA HAD KISSED his mouth and his hairless, thin-ribbed chest. She remembered this even as she handed over the first of her letters, the first of the swastika-embossed envelopes. A small and brittle laughter at the memory, even as she released her hold on the paper, gave this woman—fat as a pickle, wrapped in a body-length lilac scarf—notification of her husband's death. The poor, obese, oblong woman—she'd smiled at the girl's hopeful face—and Maria felt guilty about this later, lying in bed, her knees swollen as cabbages.

—WAGNER? NO. IT can't be. Ruth Wagner?

—That's what it says.

—Open it.

—To Ruth Wagner, registered post, hand-delivered, certified agent. That's me.

—They use the guillotine, you know.

—Bill for execution . . . the usual . . . Alfons Wagner, husband of Ruth.

Hulbert put his hand to his face, rubbed his forehead with the tips of his fingers. This was a gesture he had learned without noticing, somehow, and now—he dreamed it, the weariness on him like an overcoat, a fully inhabited second skin.

FOR FLOUR, FOR bread, for soap. Soap was the best, but the rarest. No one had permission to take a bath, anyway, except the rumors of a few officers, once a week. The rumors were always the cleanest. Maria and Hulbert, of course, had no bathtub, no plumbing at all in this cellar where they'd squatted, where no one else had come in five weeks. The *Mietskasernen,* the rental barracks, had become a great emptiness, bare as the war itself. The spiders were their sole inhabitants.

Look, Maria said of one in particular, a wolf spider that was poised in the half-dark, a meter from their pillow. *It's listening. It wants to talk, Hulbert. Say something to it. It wants a conversation.*

—COUGH NOW. YOU can cough now. Go on. I don't mind.

He turned to Hulbert. The prisoner he'd kicked was still writhing on the ground. The Unteroffizier unbuttoned his pistol's leather holster.

—But I need this quickly, *Spargel*, so hurry. You're the only one who can leave, as you can see. . . .

AT THE WAR'S BEGINNING, still only a child, he had crumpled into panic whenever he saw the black uniforms, the seamed wool trousers that tucked so neatly into the oversized boots. Now, he'd learned to negotiate their space, to say *yes* quickly, to leave as soon as he could. For some reason, these soldiers seemed to love children.

RUTH WAGNER MARKED another day off on her calendar. It had been five months, now. She stood at her fourth floor window, looked out over Berlin. What had been an awful view—the back of an appliance warehouse, red brick and a shadow of a fire escape—was now a panorama of rubble.

One chimney jutted from the wet ruin, solitary as a lamppost.

Ruth's building was the last on her block.

In the center of the street, a crater dug a five-meter pit in the concrete; in the crater's center was an overturned sofa—green and yellow, a noxious plaid.

Ruth stood at the window and rolled the pen between her palms. She sighed and leaned forward against the glass, thinking of her husband.

—HOW OLD ARE we, Maria?

—Twelve, yesterday. Twelve, still, today.

The asparagus can dig?

—Who said that?

—DOES IT HURT?

The Unteroffizier had raised his hands in the air and paused, looked quickly to the left and to the right, a conductor initiating the orchestra of slaves.

—Do they feel it, you mean?

—Yes, sir.

—Of course, lieutenant, but not like us. Take that boy over there.

He pointed with his pistol, the barrel still warm.

—If I shot him, he would feel his life, his consciousness, slipping away. Even if for only an instant, he'd feel it. This corpse, he didn't feel a thing. Not like we would, not like that boy would.

AND HE'D SEEN Maria at the alley's end, walking, of all things, towards him. Seeing her face, her beautiful, luminous face, he began to run, to sprint, towards her. The heaviness on his shoulders—the section of tusk, thick and pearled and another knot, a new part of his chordate spine—dissipated, clattered against him easily, weightless as canvas or heat.

—HOW IS THE tusk coming, *Spargel*?

—Almost free of the ground, sir.

He sat on an older man's shoulder. A prisoner. Bony hands on his thighs, the hold of a skeletal structure. Hulbert sawed back and forth, curls of the ivory rising from the tusk's seam. It was a cold November day, and his own hands? They hurt as they wrapped around the blade of the saw. They were pink and moist, and they were sweating, making the handle damp.

DID THE DEVIL eat cabbages? He must eat cabbages, she

thought, and stirred her broth—it was all bacon fat and celery. Ruth looked at her hands; they were sagging into wrinkles, the skin was beginning to hang off of her wrists, towards the tips of her fingers. The skin, once clean and colored like a lump of putty, was now spotted and creased and stained. She stared at the steam from the boiling water and then she heard the knock at her door.

—What are you doing?

—No, what are *you* doing?

They kissed, a sudden collision. Maria wasn't sure if this was what they were supposed to do—this kiss upon seeing each other unexpectedly—but she felt the now-familiar press of Hulbert's lips and could think of nothing else. She touched his chin with her mouth, ran the flat of her tongue over the faint hairs that had only begun to accumulate there, beneath his lip. She held his shoulders in her hands and licked his eyes—they had closed now—tasted the salt of his skin, its sharpness.

—It can't be.

—It is. Look. Read it.

—Board per day: 1.50. Transport to Brandenburg Prison: 12.90. Execution of sentence: 158.18. Fee for death sentence: 300.00. There must be over five hundred marks here—

—474.84. Exactly. It's almost always the same.

—But we can't give this to her.

—It's a bill. She has to pay it—

—For her own husband's execution?

—Hully, it's my work. I'm lucky. Like this, at least we can eat.

THE UNTEROFFIZIER HAD just shot another man. This one had been trying to escape. In the pucker of November cold, he licked the barrel of his pistol, felt its sear against his tongue. He always did this when he fired the Luger.

How beautiful, how the bodies steam, he thought, *after they die. This is truly a beautiful, and, of course, such a necessary, art.* He turned to his subordinate officer.

—Is that boy back yet? Has he delivered my tusk to Celeste?

RUTH WALKED TO the door. She hated the door, wished it didn't exist. People were always leaving through doors—that's all they were good for—and Ruth hated people leaving. Once you lost someone you loved, who you truly loved, she realized, you never wanted to see another door again. Because there was always a last time, a last departure, a last aperture to traverse. She undid the latch with her spotted hands. Opening it slightly, she saw the space of nothing at eye level and then, at her ankles, leaning against the drawn in frame. . . . What was it? Was it petrified wood? Was it a rock, a jagged rock, placed here as a joke? She leaned down to look.

—I HAVE AN idea, Hully.

He was sitting on the curb, drawing his hands back and forth through the dirty water of the gutter.

—What is it?

—Let's take your tusk. I know what we can do with it. I know where it should go.

RUTH PUT THE tusk—unwieldy, heavy, caked with blood—in her fireplace. *Of all the things,* she thought, *of all the things to find on your doorstep.* She smiled. *And I didn't even know they shed.* Ruth brushed its texture with her hand. It was the first surface she'd touched in such a long time, she realized, that seemed like it actually was there.

IF THE DEVIL wore cologne, the workers muttered.

THE S-BAHN WAS BOMBED OUT AGAIN, so they had to walk. The dust from the city was horrific; it choked you, coated your clothes and face as soon as you left a building. Hulbert and Maria worked outside all day—by night, their lungs were sore and their faces webbed with dust. Near the *Mietskasemen,* in the park with a few last, swollen linden, Hulbert stepped on a nail. It went cleanly through his shoe and his skin, went deep into the flesh of his foot. He folded downward, crooked, off-balance.

—Maria.

They'd been walking for almost an hour. They were close to home. Everything around them looked like a photograph of itself, all granulate and shadow. He was crooked, off-balance; he began to topple.

—Maria.

And she was there, of course, her swollen knees and her tired, stiff body. And then she had his shoe in her hands and she was putting pressure on the dirty, bleeding skin. His foot was stitched with scabs and raw abrasions and now, this solid puncture. The blood was oddly pale, colored like a mouth.

—Maria, it's not stopping.

His voice was thin. He was so tired.

—It's not stopping.

—Quiet, Hully, hush. It will stop.

She kissed his sweat-thickened hair. Behind her, the city was burning. The smoke was burgeoning upward, humming softly and rising, a kindling of marrow and of bone.

A Letter from the Margins of the Year

This past September, when our annual anxiety over the Red Sox had reached its peak, and every bar seemed to be filled, as usual, with middle-aged men whose fathers (God rest their souls) had died with the name Bill Buckner on their lips, I awoke, on a regular basis, to the singing of a wild bird.

It was a robin, actually, a small thing with a terra-cotta chest and two bright, inordinately attentive eyes—and it lived for a few tumultuous days in a cereal box on my living room table. With the first light through the bay windows it would begin its busy song, clear and sonorous and persistent as an alarm clock. The whole situation was, for me, extremely unusual.

You see, I've never had a particular fondness for birds. A single zoology course as an undergrad convinced me of this much: Wild animals are just that—*wild.* They migrate; we domesticate. They burrow into the ground; we build above it. We tend to shower compulsively, to slather ourselves in aftershave and perfume and anti-perspirant; they harbor a cornucopia of parasitic mites in their skin and hair. The bull elk, for example, will wallow in a paste of mud and urine in order to make himself more attractive during mating season. Let's preserve their difference—I've always said—preserve their habitat and their wilderness reserves, their feasts of shrubs or carrion. I'll just take my house on the end of the Green Line, my well-scrubbed, suburban eateries, my propensity to vacuum the hardwood floors twice a week, and we can both coexist in peace. End of story.

BUT IN MY DREAM I am chopping garlic. The cloves stick to my hands as I split their husks. The knife is sharp and slices well but they still stick—clinging to my skin like disobedient children. I have been singing a song: Bing Crosby's *White Christmas,* but I can't remember the words that aren't in the title. So I hum. The knife cuts the garlic and I'm transferring it to the stovetop, humming. Now the garlic is sizzling in the pan. The cloves are twirling in the spitting oil. They spell out my name: Stanley Albertson. They sizzle and pop and arrange themselves into the numbers of my age: first the four, then the nine. The garlic is introducing itself to me, I realize, but it owns my name and my age. Horrified, I see that I have sliced and cooked the tips of my fingers by mistake.

I wake up. It's four in the morning and the moon is visible and full in the window. I've been trying, I see now, to introduce myself. I am a professor of modern British literature at a large, private university in Boston. I cherish Chaucer, but I adore Adorno.

From bed, I look out at the unapologetic moon. I sort through the scraps of myself—tapping draft after draft onto the smooth page of the cool night air. What should I say? What's most critical? There is, for example, my pathological fear of porcelain. Or my irredeemable fascination with the circus. I own, at last count, twelve vinyl recordings of Mahler's Ninth Symphony. I drink tea with milk and strawberry jam. Also though, and perhaps most importantly, I have never, even remotely, wanted to perform in a Broadway revival of the musical *Grease.*

ON SEPTEMBER 8TH, 1998, the morning when my tenure was guaranteed in writing, I was surprised by what I felt—by the ways in which the emotion wasn't quite understandable, how it lay somewhere between happiness and regret. I folded the notice twice—folded this paper that already felt like an artifact—and slipped it into the chest pocket of my blazer.

It was a Tuesday, and I had office hours scheduled for the morning. My students were particularly confused, it seemed, by the poems of Gerard Manley Hopkins. At least this is what their email said, email which included, more often than not, various pleas for an extension of term-paper deadlines. Somehow, however, no matter how confused my students were, my office hours tended to be barren. Quiet. A full measure of silence. And there was also a Sox doubleheader.

I took a shot of the whiskey I kept in my desk and waited for twenty minutes. No one came. Still wearing the blazer, I left my small office and wandered down the hall to the department secretary.

—John, I'm feeling ill.

—Already? It's only September.

—I know. But I'm terribly sick. Yellow fever, perhaps. Or possibly malaria.

—I see. Cancel your office hours, then, this afternoon?

Among the advantages of my school—its greatest advantage, in my eyes—is its location on the banks of the Charles, its proximity to Fenway Park. Within seconds of leaving the department, I was on Commonwealth, negotiating the intricate traffic towards Brookline. It was about an hour before the first pitch. The gates would be open. Batting practice would be half-finished.

The park during batting practice is a clean space. It is a space like you see in the movies—when the director needs to ground the story in a setting, needs an atmosphere into which the characters rise, gradual and detailed, an overture. There is a scrap of conversation, or a shirt worn misbuttoned, or lipstick on a collar. There is a distant stare, or an uneasy laugh, or dramatic music played far away, over the PA speakers. The anticipation builds; the fans fall in with a gradual flow.

I spotted a scalper, motioned that I needed a ticket. He lumbered towards me.

—How many you need? I got first base, third base, bleachers. Ten over face value, both games.

—Ten over? But it's the Tigers. I can shop around.

—Eight over, just for you. How many you need? A family pack? You from Detroit? You look like you're from Detroit.

I smiled.

—Born and raised. Live there now. Work for Chevy. And so the Tigers will lose two, and I'll end up depressed, like always. That's why I'll give you five over, for one seat.

—Just one? I can't sell them off in singles. Seven over, then, since it's just one.

At that moment, I am unsure what I was thinking. Mostly, of course, I was preoccupied by the scalper. He was sweating profusely, despite the cold air, and he had a large mole growing from the corner of his mouth. It looked like a miniature marshmallow—faded and swollen and possibly infected at its edges. But as I opened my wallet, and he peeled one ticket from the pile he was clutching in his meaty fist, I paused, trapped on the edge of an idea.

—Okay. I tell you what. I changed my mind. Give me two, and I'll give you seven over.

—Now that's more like it. You sure you don't want three? Maybe four, even? I got four, right behind the plate.

By now, I recognize that I'd known, since the very moment I received the confirmation of tenure in the morning's campus mail, exactly what I was going to do. I'd known before I picked up the receiver of the pay phone. I'd known before I dialed her number, a number I'd memorized but never called in the first days of the separation, a number that had stayed in my mind even though I'd willed myself to forget it. I'd known before I heard the click of the machine and the beginning of her voice, her sad-sounding voice that promised she'd return my call if, and only if, I left a number. I'd known before I hesitated, before I waited three full seconds to begin speaking, before I told the machine, without any preamble, that I had an extra ticket to both Red Sox games today, to both games of the doubleheader. Before I said that I wanted to see her, that I missed her, somehow, that I wondered how she was doing, that she could send Samantha if she wanted to, that I would leave the tickets at will call, that these seats shouldn't be wasted, didn't she think, after all.

I FEEL THAT, BY THIS POINT, I SHOULD CLARIFY MY RELATIONSHIP WITH BASEBALL. It is the great cliché of New England sports fans that Fenway is our cathedral—that it is the only place where we receive a full and honest reprisal for our sins, which must be many, and variegated, and grim. I've never been able to count myself a follower of this argument—compelling as it is—mostly because of the bowling alley that is located in Fenway's basement. Any church with a bowling alley in its basement must serve a God with a better sense of humor than the one I've come to believe in.

But the argument is not a bad one. There is a clean, nearly sacred joy in the infinity of the foul lines. There is a ladder on the Green Monster that is in play—a metaphor if I've ever seen one—and the outfield scoreboard is still operated by hand. The scent of the grass and the dirt, if it is a wet Spring day, can remind you, in a way, of incense. The game is timeless in the same way that religious ritual is timeless; it is bound only by the constraint of the innings. There is the noise of praise, which is often rabid. And, as with any good church, there is opportunity for lament, as year after year a goal is not quite achieved.

I remember three images from these two games, three moments of sight that impress themselves upon me above all others:

1) The first pitch. I was sitting immediately behind an obese man wearing a scarlet-colored wig. Despite the cold weather, he was shirtless, a fact which betrayed a swath of hair, broad as the back of a boar, that stretched from his neck to his waistline. From time to time, the man would turn around and wave at the rest of the crowd, begging them to yell, to scream, to make more noise. He had an enormous red stocking on the front of his stomach, laboriously stenciled into place with what seemed to be (and I could only guess) lipstick. When the Red Sox lost the first game, he unleashed a torrent of obscenities. I saw several parents cover the ears of their children, which seemed to me a futile gesture, since the kids couldn't stop looking, wouldn't stop looking, were rapturously in love.

2) The light in the second game. The man with the wig disappeared. But the light—the light became something unexpected, something gauzy, something silver. It fell in great ropes

from the stanchions. Thousands of electric bulbs, encased in shining cups of steel. Fog was coming in off the harbor. A few rows away from me, an elderly couple were having a conversation, and breath moved from their mouths in steady vapor. Linda wasn't coming, I realized—of course she wasn't coming—and I proceeded to the concessions stand, ordered myself a king-size lite beer.

3) When the Sox were retired in order in the bottom of the ninth, ending the dismal doubleheader, the few thousand remaining fans stood and sighed—a collective, emphatic standing and sighing—and began to muddle towards the exits. I sat there, sipping the last of the beer and eating the occasional peanut. I mashed the shells with my teeth, reducing and crushing their fibers to a salty pulp. The night was already cold. The cars would be covered in frost, in a thin silver sheet, an opaque overcoat to the glass of the windshields. I imagined the warmth of the train, felt already the way the heat would hit me as I entered the station, a sudden rush of air.

I hadn't intended to be the last fan to leave the park. But as the ushers spread out to clear us from the stands, and the custodians began to work their way through the day's sticky detritus, I felt a growing need to stay, to sink into the seat, to remain here, a little drunk, and watch the stadium. The cleaning crew was large—hundreds of people—and they worked quickly, pulling trash bins behind them on wheels as they went along. A certain silence descended—a silence like any small street in winter—but here it was full, filled with space, filled with people. After some time like this, I felt a tap on my shoulder.

—Sir?

The usher was looking at me quizzically.

—The players will exit through the clubhouse near Gate C,

sir, if you're interested in autographs.

IT WAS DARK when I left the stadium. I'd forgotten a book in my office, a book I was supposed to review over the weekend, and I made my way back towards my building. As I neared its entrance, neared the broad brick façade that flattened against the street, I noticed some sort of motion in the gutter beneath a streetlight. It was a small twitching—the movement of something that was clearly alive.

The robins were born out of season, my daughter later informed me, and that was what made them so unusual. Four of them, and they had tumbled helplessly from their ledge to the pavement, swept up in the fall of their nest, suddenly motherless. Three of them were dead—I saw this as soon as I towered over the tragic little scene—but one was stubbornly still living, huddled in the middle of the nest, perched atop the feathery lump of its dead siblings. It bobbed its head wildly, suspicious of everything, and opened its beak to hiss at my descending hand. It was unsure, I suppose, if I was food or a mortal enemy.

I'd never held a bird in my hands, and though I knew that its bones would be hollow, I was immediately surprised by how light, how close to nothing, this animal was. What was I supposed to do? I felt like an interloper, an intruder in the arena of its death, and I wanted immediately to put it back down, to leave it in the gutter and go about my business. But it was looking at me—quietly, now—and I could feel the smallest details of its feathers against my skin.

For the next hour I held it like that, cupped in my palm, half the size of my entire hand, weighing less than a few ounces. The train was crowded, and I had to stand against the back wall of the compartment. I held the bird close to my body, and no one seemed to notice or, if they noticed, didn't seem to care. Once, late on a Thursday on the Green Line downtown, I entered the car to find a mule—entirely calm and docile—tethered by a rope to the overhead handrail. There was only one other passenger, an elderly woman, and she was staring at her reflection in the window. This animal looked at me, forlorn in its mulish way, and chewed on something, perhaps its own mouth. I rode the train for ten minutes. Several passengers got on and off. No one said a word.

WHEN LINDA LEFT ME, she also left our dog. Our dog was an Irish wolfhound, a huge and hairy beast that we had, in a moment of dubious inspiration, named Finnegan. Unlike most dogs, Finnegan didn't greet me at the door when I came home. He wasn't happy, or bucolic, or light-hearted. He never showed any affection, really, only occasional hunger. He did, however, defend his territory.

I flicked on the lights in the living room. Within seconds, the scent of the bird had attracted his attention. He rose from his place on the couch—head first, yawning, then the shoulders, then the hips—and padded over towards me. I was frozen in the entryway, unsure of what to do. Would he try to eat the bird if I put it on the floor? Was the bird still alive? I checked. It was sleeping, curled in my hand, breathing regularly.

—Hello, Finn. Good dog. I've got live cargo, here, Finnegan, clear the way.

Over the course of the next hour I tried to fashion, as best I could, a shelter for the tiny thing. I realize now, of course, that I should have called the Humane Society, or the university's veterinary college, or anyone remotely familiar with the development of wild birds. But that night, slightly drunk and brimming with a sense of stewardship, I only concentrated on what I could do, on how I could help this particular animal, just me. How I could fix the terrible injustice of office buildings, of exposed ledges, of the wind and the descent to the cement. Still holding the bird in my left hand, I grabbed a kitchen knife with my right, and used it to slice open a throw pillow. I cut a cereal box in half, too, and arranged the stuffing carefully inside. Was I neglecting anything? Should I try to feed the bird? What would I feed it? I nudged the robin with the edge of my thumb. No response. I set it in the center of the makeshift nest, then carried the whole package to the living room. I placed it on the coffee table.

Finnegan was immediately there, but I stared at him meaningfully, raising my eyebrows into the implication of a threat. He backed off, paced a few feet away, sprawled on the ground. The bird wasn't moving, really, save for the rise and fall of its pale red chest. I stared at the box, thinking as little as possible. The reflection of the whole scene was visible in the glass of the living room windows. Had I turned on the lights? Tired, forgetting the order of things, I fell asleep on the couch, lulled unconscious by the rhythm of my own breathing.

This time, I awoke with a headache. And the doorbell. I woke up with the doorbell, a pounding, concussive alarm, and I was stumbling into the hallway, and my hand was on the door, and I squinted out onto the porch to see my daughter, my nine-year-old Samantha, smoking a cigarette. Or, no, that wasn't right—it was just the steam of her breath in the cold morning, not a cigarette, and she was saying:

—Can I come in, or what?

Right. It was her customary weekend visit, and then I heard

a scrambling sound behind me and I remembered, much too late, the infant bird. And even as I began cursing, and running back into the living room, I could hear the beginning of a birdsong, somehow muffled, and a certain hesitant whimpering, and then both Samantha and I were in the house and confronted with an interesting scene.

Finnegan had taken advantage of my absence to snatch up the bird, stuffing and all, and pad away towards the kitchen. He had apparently stopped in mid-step, however, as the bird—roused from its stupor by the light and the saliva from a dog's tongue—began to sing. It was as pleasant of a melody as I've ever heard from the beak of a bird, and seemed to be somehow in harmony with Finnegan's whimper. The sensation of a live singing bird in his mouth was, I now believe, beyond the range of his understandable experiences.

—Dad? What is that?

—That's Finnegan, honey.

—But in his mouth?

—Oh, that. Well, that's an A-flat, I think.

WE SPENT THE WEEKEND caring for it, our lives reduced to a ridiculous simplicity. Samantha connected to the Internet and found instructions on how to rehabilitate a wild bird. Laboriously exact, she heated one quart of water in the microwave, then added a teaspoon of salt and three teaspoons of sugar. Every twenty minutes, earnest as any practicing veterinarian, Samantha would rouse the robin and feed it from an eyedropper. She would use her hands to steer the bird's beak towards the solution, careful to give it only the smallest pressure. Despite these attentions, the robin didn't seem overly healthy, or active, or chipper. *The prognosis isn't good*, Samantha told me that night. I nodded. When, I wondered, had she learned the word prognosis?

On Sunday morning, though, the robin sang. We had slept in the living room—I'd given her the couch and taken the floor—and we'd locked Finnegan in the master bedroom. With the first light through the windows, the robin was singing, and the sound of it was unexpected and wonderful—a certain, if somewhat modest, wildness.

I lay on the floor in the shell of my sleeping bag. It was a strange music and, up close, you could hear the components of the song that were usually stolen by distance, the stutters of breath and the grain of its voice. I watched my daughter's face, struck by how beautiful she was, waiting there, entirely still, waiting for the song to end.

LINDA'S CAR was precisely on time, as usual, idling out in the driveway at seven p.m. on Sunday night. Samantha kissed my cheek and, with careful instructions on how to care for the bird, she ran out the door. My daughter—restored to me for two brief days—was gone again. I was alone in the house—a condition that I still couldn't bear—and I walked over to the table, sat on the floor close to the robin. I looked at it. Its little eyes looked back at me. *What now?* It seemed to ask. I shook my head. Under no circumstances, I said out loud, will I talk to a bird.

SAMANTHA was there the next morning.

6:54 a.m., and Linda waited outside, present only as the distant rattle of a motor. I answered the door in my bathrobe. Samantha shouldered her way around me—using her backpack to gain leverage—and checked on the robin. It was awake. She fed it some of the water, though it had cooled overnight and the sugar and salt had condensed at the bottom of the bowl.

—It sang about half an hour ago, I said.

—Did you come down? It was probably lonely.

—I was asleep, Sam. By the time I woke up it was done. Don't you have to be at school?

—Mom's taking me. Bye, dad. See you tomorrow.

I watched her leave again.

On Tuesday I was somewhat prepared. I pre-heated the water in the microwave, made myself a cup of coffee and a bagel. I handed Samantha the eye-dropper as soon as she came through the door.

By Wednesday I was sophisticated. I dug an old, hand-held tape-recorder from the closet and, still concealed by darkness, crept downstairs into the living room. I pressed record as soon as the bird started singing. For ten minutes, the cassette captured this common ritual, this celebration of the new day, that was so unlike our mechanical approximation—the petulant alarm clock, the whiny, insistent snooze button.

I handed Samantha the tape as she was feeding the robin, placed it quietly on the corner of the table and stepped back a few feet.

—What's this? She asked, turning her head only slightly, still concentrating on the bird.

—Play it for your mother in the car, I said.

That night I came back late from the office. It had been a good day, with little work and only a few drinks for lunch. I had two messages on my answering machine. I pressed play and suddenly, suddenly I was listening to Linda's voice:

The Transcript:

Call one. Machine repeats time of call and day of week.

—Hi, Stan. It's me, Linda. You know…

Nervous sound, either cough or laugh.

—Listen…

Pause.

—Samantha loves what you did for the, um, the robin. It's all she talks about, you know…

Another pause.

—Listen. So I got your message the other day, and I wasn't going to call you back, and I thought it was so irresponsible. But… I mean, it was ridiculous… But, but now I don't know. Listen. I have two tickets, and I'll leave them at Will Call. This Friday. To make up for it. You know. Samantha has a sitter. Call me back.

Dial tone.

Call two. Machine repeats time of call and day of week.

—Hi, Stan. It's me again. Linda. It's two tickets to the Red Sox. That's what I meant. Friday's game against the Mariners. I don't think I said that. And I'll leave them at Will Call under your name. I'll leave one, I mean.

Pause.

—I'd like to see you.

Unidentifiable noise in background.

—Okay. Bye.

I reached my hand out towards the sliding glass door. My

fingertips touched the glass, four soft points of contact. The coolness from the September day moved from the panel and into my skin.

SHE ARRIVED in the second inning. Tim Wakefield was pitching, I believe, and I was enjoying the knuckleball. It moved with a simple grace, plush and opulent, entirely unexpected. I was thinking of nothing and she was there, standing at the mouth of the aisle.

There is a singular emotion that is experienced, I believe, by the lonely and questionably alcoholic college professor encountering his estranged wife for the first time in slightly over a year. I would describe this emotion in detail if I could remember it. I really would. But instead, I'll have to substitute a recipe for beet soup:

Linda's Mother's Borscht.

Serves 4.

1.5 pounds beef chuck, cut up
1.5 quarts water
4 medium beets, cooked and sliced
2 celery stalks, diced
1 onion, minced
salt and pepper
.25 cups dairy sour cream
2 tablespoons all-purpose flour
1 egg

Put meat in kettle and add water.
Bring to boil and simmer, covered, for 1 1/2 - 2

hours, or until meat is almost tender.

Add beets, celery, and onion, Cook for about 30 minutes.

Season.

Blend sour cream, flour and egg.

Stir into soup, bring again to boil.

Serve in soup bowls on boiled potatoes. Torment son-in-law with absurdly large portions.

LINDA AND I DISCUSSED this recipe in detail during the fifth inning. Somehow, she had begun talking about her mother—now dead—and the first Thanksgiving I'd spent at their house, when I'd been expected to consume, without warning and at all hours of the day, bowl after bowl of steaming borscht.

As Linda talked, I watched her mouth shape the familiar letters and phrases, watched it give voice to the rattle of language. It was a funny mouth. Turned down at one side, it hesitated over vowels, paused to elongate them, as if this whole business—the production of language—was a slightly painful process. She had applied her lipstick in a rush. The streak of it was crooked over her lips. I looked seriously at her while she talked, all the while listening solely to her body, to the fragile articulations of her hips and elbows. She was a photograph of herself, too cinematic to understand. My head was full of ridiculous questions.

WE LEFT in the top of the eighth. I still don't know who won. But there was something simple in the way we left without knowing, in the way we stood up and walked out of Fenway before everyone else. And we were together, the two of us, and alone. *This is extremely rare,* I kept thinking to myself. In the days following the initial separation, I had swayed into Barnes & Noble and read magazine article after magazine article about the odds of a marriage surviving a split. Bitterness on both sides, the journalists seemed to agree, would make even a partial reconciliation difficult.

And yet, and yet, here we were, almost accidentally, not talking about anything important, but walking, walking together out onto the street, down through the belly of the stadium and into the bright air. There was possibility in this. Even though we were only going to the subway—to the station where our lines would diverge—we were still walking and talking, making a certain music with the sounds of our voices. Linda was beautiful, really, walking beside me, and then she snagged her heel on the cement and stumbled forward into a lamppost, and she was half-laughing, a little sad, and I was marveling at that sound, low and thick like I remembered it, almost marvelous in the way it was exactly like my memory.

—It's broken, she said, her voice changing. Damn. I broke it.

I must not have reacted to this in the right way, or maybe I was smiling slightly, because she was immediately upset—so quickly and immediately upset—and her voice rose in pitch, skittered up the register.

—You think this is funny? I can barely walk and you think it's funny. Damn heels.

—No, no. I wasn't, I just—

—You have to make it a joke at my expense, don't you Stanley, you think it's all—

—Linda, no, you have it all wrong. That's not what I meant.

I have long believed that the life-motions of an alcoholic are true to the mechanical-motions of modern speed. The roller coaster, the acceleration off the runway, the 0 to 60 in a few fragile seconds—all of these have their equivalent in a drunk's daily life. Lurch and rattle, with bright colors at the edges. Linda and I walked the remaining two blocks in silence. Then, at the entrance to the station, she turned to face me. She took my lapel in her hand, letting her fingernails clatter over the metal of the zipper.

—Are you going to meetings?

I looked at her. I wanted to lie but I couldn't.

—No, I said. No, I'm not.

Linda nodded. She let go of the edge of my coat. She hugged me briefly—with no strength in her arms, it seemed—and then she skittered away, swallowed by the station entrance.

I WAS HOME IN TWENTY MINUTES. On the front steps and then through the door—briskly, briskly—and instinctively I knew that something was wrong.

It wasn't the dog. I could hear him up in the bedroom, whimpering and clawing at the door. There had been no burglary. Nothing was missing or displaced. I walked around the corner and into the living room, where I nearly stepped on the body of the bird—on a disorganized mass of wings on the hardwood. It wasn't moving. For the second time in a week, I lifted the robin, wondering at its smallness, at its barely believable nothing. This time, however, it didn't rise, unexpected, from my hands.

At first I didn't know what to do. How could it just die? I was unprepared. But then, my mind began working in its circuitous way and, after some time, I had a rough plan of action.

I worked all night at the funeral. A late-night trip to the Big K had produced some black crepe paper—a pre-Halloween sale—and I strung the stuff from the doorway to the kitchen cabinets. I lit silver candles, too, and placed them at all the corners of the living room. I turned the cereal box into a two-handled bier. I leaned a shovel against the door to my tiny backyard.

Despite everything, Linda was still punctual, and Samantha made it through the door with her customary speed. She stopped, though, when she saw me in the center of the candle-filled room, wearing a black shirt, black pants and, for lack of anything else, a black cooking apron. She frowned.

—What's going on? You look crazy, dad.

—We are gathered here today, I intoned, dropping the pitch of my voice just as I had rehearsed. We are gathered here today to witness the end of a great warrior, the slain Agamemnon, valiant of Mycenae. I have brought forth the long, rich bones of bulls and goats—

—Dad?

—To sacrifice before his body, after the internment of which we will begin the funeral games.

—Funeral? Wait. Funeral for the bird?

Sam was around the couch and at the coffee table, and she was crying and it was suddenly much more difficult to continue. I picked up the Homer and began reading aloud and somehow Samantha understood, understood the ridiculous thing I was trying to do, and she sat there with her hands on her knees, hovering next to the robin. After some time I stopped reading and outside I could hear that her mother had turned off the motor of the car. Linda was out in the driveway but she wouldn't come in, she would only wait, unaware. And so my daughter and I carried the bird into the backyard and began digging—quietly—through the matted roots of the wet morning grass.

Like a Fish, Like An Eel

You're walking in old Riga, near the Fish Market, along a street fringed with coral colored buildings. The architecture is a broken geometry, Soviet beside baroque, a slab of concrete roof beside an ornamented roof of red tiles. And there—the three domes of the Market, its scent overwhelming even a block away, a musk of brine and organic rot that is exaggerated by the cold March wind. You rub your ears to keep warm. The skin of your face tingles wherever it's exposed. You open your mouth and feel the air sweeten along your tongue, cap each of your teeth.

A stray dog sleeps in the doorway to a Russian butcher's shop. He must be dreaming of the meat—whole carcasses of it hanging in the window near his head. You hesitate for a moment, afraid of waking him. You read a label. Thirty-one dollars, you calculate, for an entire side of beef. Your reflection seems fat in the glass, framed as it is by the loping strokes of the Cyrillic.

It's two a.m. You've had dinner at your godmother's house and now you're carrying a smoked chicken. She pressed it into your hands as you left, saying: Take, take and eat. It could have been a bomb. You would have smiled even then, grateful and polite, your Latvian overly-formal, obviously learned from books. *Thank you for these fine explosives*, you would have said. *I will try my best to use them tonight.*

A CARNIVAL BARKER. His voice is wet and resonant, slapping and echoing over the cobblestones like a just-caught fish. He's passing out handbills that read:

Le Magicien Americain Extraordinaire!
Comme un Poisson!
Comme une Arguille!
Gratuit!

(Les donations sont acceptées)

—*Mesdames, mesdemoiselles, et messieurs!* He says, and begins his promotion, his French thickly accented, a walking stick twirling in his hands, tapping against the ground with each step of his scuffed black shoes.

It is Sunday, May 20th, 1908. Houdini's in Paris. At noon, he will leap from a bridge over the Seine, his hands shackled behind him, his ankles bound by thick iron chains. His body will sink into the cold river, a white blur swallowed by the sedimented murk. His wife and her assistant will wait on the bridge, looking nervously downstream, scanning the surface for any human form. The crowd will be silent. From time to time someone will cough. As the minutes elapse, the police will fan out through the spectators. He's dead! Someone will shout. *Houdini est mort!* And Beatrice, his beautiful young wife, will begin to weep into her handkerchief. She will faint, falling into the arms of Hardeen, her assistant, who will catch her carefully, cautious not to disturb the precise arrangement of her luxurious hair.

Never read the guidebooks. They give you ideas like this. The Fish Markets are liveliest, yours said, at three in the morning, when the fish come in. *I am a fool*, you think, as you cross Kalpaku Plaza and pass a row of warehouses, mute in the darkness. *I will be bludgeoned and murdered. I will be skinned and sold as tuna.*

You come to the back gate of the building. There is no guard on duty. Fifty meters away there is a row of boxy trucks—Soviet-made cousins to American eighteen-wheelers—and hundreds of workers, a thick buzz of men, unloading long boxes from beds of ice. The smell of exhaust rises into the air, sweet roses. Last week, a Norwegian freighter spilled six tons of chemical waste into the Baltic, just north of the Estonian border. Are the fish glowing slightly, you wonder, or is that just the reflection of the lighting along their skin?

—*Ej, puisi! Boy! Tu mekleji darbu?* You looking for work?

It is the foreman—a fat, club-nosed man who's wearing all denim. You are surprised—he appears so suddenly, holding a clipboard and roaring at you in Latvian tinged by a thick Russian accent. He comes closer, stops, looks at you like he's beginning to think. You want to explain it all—the guidebook, the walk, the lure of the briny smelling fish—but you just tighten your lips and nod your head. The foreman points to one of the trucks.

—Just in from Liepaja. River eel.

You place your smoked chicken near the fence, and soon you're unloading the boxes with the others, fourth in a chain of six, passing the icy cardboard along towards the entrance. They've wheeled out the scales—huge iron plates caked with iridescent fish skin—and two more men split open the boxes when they arrive at the doors. Each fish is weighed individually—you see as much as you can while you're lifting—and someone seems to be adding up the weight of the eels on an abacus. Your hands begin to chafe and ache with the cold water. You are the only one without gloves, but no one offers you anything, no one seems to have an extra pair, and the rhythm of the labor surges along. Thirty minutes pass. Your arms begin to cramp, shivers of pain spiraling through your triceps, and then suddenly the truck is empty, there are no more eels, your work is done.

Two of the laborers from the line leap into the cargo bay and begin to sweep out the ice. The foreman appears again, materializing from somewhere, and he's smoking a brown cigarette. He has a handful of items: a stack of banknotes, a bottle of vodka, a number of small paper bags, heavy with something. There seems to be a procedure here—payment by the truck. The others present themselves, one by one, and receive their pay. First the vodka, one mouthful, as much as they can drink. Then the money—two *lati*, or seventy cents. Then the eels—three of them in a sack, their bodies long and sinewy, you can see, beneath the wet paper surface.

The foreman approaches you and again you want to explain, to say that you don't belong here, that you don't need the money, that it's all a mistake. But then he's standing in front of you—you can't escape him—and you can see the hair on his knuckles, and the lip of the bottle is wet with saliva as it touches the skin of your lips.

UNDERWATER, Houdini struggles to undo the chains, to slide them over his wrists and move free. His face bulges with the he cuffs, the veins on the sides of his temples rising e skin. Is it the taste of the water, oily and sour—somehow leaking into his mouth—that makes him move so furiously, his muscles buckling and contracting to ward off death? Or does he even dive into the water? Does the illusion happen earlier, on the lip of the bridge, before his mass seems to fall, trailing chains and ropes like a wounded comet? And his wife, does she have pepper in her sleeves? Are those genuine tears? Are his handcuffs even real? How is the entire crowd deceived? He practices each night, someone says, how to turn himself into smoke. He imagines his spine as a wick. And then, as if scripted, a vendor walks by selling chestnuts—they are roasted and steaming in the cool early summer day.

As a boy in Appleton, Wisconsin, before he formally changed his name, Ehrich Weiss worked in the dairy barns, rising at three to be at work by four. Even in summer the mornings were cold and his work was slow—bringing the fifteen Holsteins from their stalls to the milking barn, easing them out into the darkness without electric lamps, with only two lanterns, one in each hand. He would sing to the cows to guide them, old songs that he'd learned from his father, the Hebrew words that he didn't quite understand. He would lead the cows that way, singing until he reached the barn door, urging them on with his lantern, touching his hand to each one as she moved on through. They were always a surprise—so bony and so warm—and they never paid him any attention at all. It was his first, and in some ways, his greatest escape. He would make himself disappear. Even as he touched them, he would use his voice to turn himself into nothing. *Look*, he would think, *I'm Robert-Houdin in the fields of Brittany. I'm performing illusions to an audience of livestock.*

Ehrich would watch as the last cow moved through the doors. The others would milk them—that wasn't his job. Instead, he would turn and walk slowly into that darkness, breathing the milky scent of the dairy mud.

WHEN YOU UNLOAD THE THIRD TRUCK you're ready for payment. You seize the vodka and drink it like water, letting it burn your throat in an eager plume. An old man with a streak of bright white hair coming out of his shirt collar stands next to you, and when his turn comes to drink, he shakes his head and glances at the floor. The foreman shrugs and drinks from the bottle himself, smiling afterwards and wiping his lips with the back of his hand. The old man looks at you then and raises his eyebrows.

—*Pirmais vakars?* He says. Is it your first night? You sure drink like it.

You nod. You look away from him then, consider the long cardboard boxes that you've helped pile along the edges of the loading dock. Where are you, really? What's the rest of the market like? You haven't had a chance to see. You've been too busy with the *foreles* and *zuti* and *lasi* and *sprati.* You turn back to the old man and ask:

—How big is this market?

—Ai, he says. Ai. So big. Enormous. Bigger than the bus station.

He pauses, still staring at you.

—Are you, by any chance, an American?

You nod again.

—Be careful, he says, if you want to keep those shoes.

And you are careful. You walk carefully through the loading bay doors and into the atrium of the market. There is a vaulted glass ceiling, you see, a distant and shining dome, home to a hundred pigeons. The floor is a muddy slate, and the building unfolds from you in what you can only imagine as an Inferno of lost souls. Maybe two hundred, three hundred vendors, yelling and laughing and cursing and counting, in Russian and Latvian and even English. Careful, you edge into it all, losing yourself in the commotion, keeping one hand on your wallet. To your left, a chef buys crabs from a barrel, holding them behind the head, avoiding the angry claws. Money moves from hand to hand, a bewildering swirl of currency and strongboxes. The tables are motley and varied. One woman sells perch from a bucket seat that has been stripped from a sedan, and you watch as ice melts out of her display and drips along the weathered red vinyl. Careful, you disappear into the crowd, imagining that despite your shoes you can somehow fit in—a chef's assistant, perhaps, sent ahead to get a jump on the morning's free-market competition.

HOUDINI'S DEATH didn't come in the midst of an escape, manacled and chained and drowned by riverwater. Instead, it came in Detroit, at Grace Hospital, of peritonitis, on the last day of October, 1926. Houdini's bequeathed his equipment and his secrets to Theodore Hardeen—Beatrice's longtime assistant—with the stipulation that they were to be burned upon Hardeen's death.

Nearly fifty years later, however, Hardeen sold the show in its entirety, unable to destroy such precious illusions. He kept only the faded promotional handbills, most of which, he found, were an ideal lining for the cages of his rabbits.

AND SO HERE YOU ARE, kicked back out into the morning air. You're wearing dirty clothes and your hair is greasy as a seal. There's a bakery on the corner—it has just opened—so you stop in and buy a loaf of bread. You sit on the corner and eat, and the hot wheat dough tastes like cod. There are scales everywhere, you realize, fish scales on your hands, on your clothes, under your fingernails. You're dizzy, you feel displaced, lost in the skin of the city. You're not yourself, you're submerged in the deepening day. You start walking in what you hope is the general direction of the hostel.

HE WAS THE HANDCUFF KING, slipping out of jail cells and metal boxes. The Police-Baffler, the King of Cards, the King of Billiard Balls, the Prince of the Air: Invented and re-invented, a new self with each day. Each day a different kind of lock—wafer, or lever, or pin-tumbler—and the pattern to opening it divulged in the tips of the fingers. Plunging through the cold riverwater, did Houdini remember the books he would read by candlelight each evening in Appleton? Joseph Bramah, *A Dissertation on the Construction of Locks?* Rudolph Ackerman, *The Secret of the Unnamable Ether?* David Bratton, *The Blue Palace of Escape: A Guide to All Types of Leaving?* Whatever the case, for him there was no question of the result. He would succeed—no matter how long his lungs had to strain against drowning. He would surface and breathe, transformed.

EVENTUALLY YOU FIND IT—the barred glass door that has been your home for the past two weeks. It's locked, and though it's early, you pound your fist against the glass, demanding loudly that someone let you in. No answer. You wait. A fat woman walks by with her schnauzer, teetering from side to side, moving like a chubby pendulum. Five minutes. You continue to pound on the door. Finally, the manager appears—his bathrobe hanging open—and he stops just short of the door and smiles. He has a row of gold teeth.

—Passport? He asks in English. Where is passport?

You smile too—it is all a wonderful farce—and your reach into your back pocket for this thing, small and dark blue and stamped with its zoo of colors. You show it to him, opening to the page with your photograph, holding the photo near your face, for comparison. But the manager suddenly looks grim. He shakes his head. Carefully, you look at the passport, wondering if it is you.

—Give it to me. I have to see it closer.

You look at the extended palm, lined with scars, twitching insistently behind the glass. The manager just stands for a while, an amused stoic, and then he launches into a torrent of Russian words—of which you only recognize *nyet*—and you feel like a nearsighted man at a subtitled movie, and then the manager is leaning down against the iron bars, his face grotesquely pinched between rows of black metal, his wet breath frosting the inside pane with a silvery condensation.

—Well? He asks. I'm waiting.

—I can't get it through the glass, you say, stupidly, as if this could somehow change his mind.

—Nine o'clock we open, he says, and starts to turns away. Somewhere, in the distance, you hear thunder.

—But it must be six. I haven't eaten—

—Nine o'clock we open, he repeats, and then he spins and he leaves you at the door, staring between the bars into the hallway. Such a nice hallway, you think. Such nice, spongy carpeting. Such nice, dry-looking walls.

There is nothing else to do, so you turn and sit on the stoop. There are few people on this street, and it is a strange sensation—being almost alone in the midst of such a large city. What should you have done differently? Should you have slept at your godmother's, like she urged you, spreading blankets on the floor near the woodstove—which is her oven and her only source of heat? Or should you have come directly here—skipped the fish market, called a taxi and paid the outrageous fare they would have charged an American? You can't decide. There it is, in front of you, Riga, the largest city in Latvia, founded in 1201 by the Teutonic Order of Knights, and all you can think about is your bed, your stiff pillow and your somewhat lumpy mattress. Sitting there on the stoop, leaning against the wrought-iron handrail, you close your eyes and, within seconds, you are asleep.

In your dream it's that morning, May 20th, 1908, on the bridge over the Seine, and it's raining. A thick, saturating wetness. You look around you; someone is selling doves from a cage, a silver cage off to one side of the crowd. The birds are white-headed, with gray and taupe wings and near-white underbellies, and they are singing with the dawn, their soft voices moving gradually through the room and guiding you awake. Didn't Houdini keep doves at the foot of his bed? You think. Didn't he stand at the cage and watch them sing each morning—the first, questioning note, followed by the gentle rattle, and then the breath in, low and private and unexpected. Sometimes, you remember now, Beatrice stood beside him, both of them naked. She would reach into the cage for one of the birds, place it on her husband's shoulder. The dove would then walk across the bridge of his back, and she would follow its path with her mouth, tasting the sweat of her husband's skin.

Beatrice is thinking briefly of these doves, your doves, of their tentative stuttering movements, of the way they differ from her tongue, abrasive instead of smooth. When Houdini performs she does this—submerges into herself until the visible world became gauzy and distant—and she waits for the reaction of the crowd. It roars, it always roars, thousands of mouths opening at once as Harry rises again, breaking suddenly through the surface to breathe the air again, just like everyone else. He clambers into a waiting rowboat, and the crowd surges forward, carries her down towards the shore. They meet at the bank, then, and she puts her hands on his bare shoulders, and the relief in her eyes is real, and they kiss, but kiss carefully, properly, decently.

And the crowd surrounds them now, a thousand French citizens, the men wearing straw hats, the women wearing bright, variegated dresses, and everyone smiles and laughs and pushes the husband and wife together. Beyond the people, Paris loafs, indifferent and graceful, part real and wrought iron, part visible and part only imagined. Isn't this all imagination anyway? She thinks, you think. Isn't it just imagination and transformation and illusion? Isn't it a sort of alchemy? Beatrice looks at Houdini and wonders about him—what does he feel when they stand there like this, surrounded and hemmed in against each other? She knows—you know—that she feels displaced, unreal, exhausted.

He's a brother of the fish, someone shouts, and she rubs her forehead with her hand, looks at the veins on her husband's neck. They bulge solidly from his skin. Could they somehow, Beatrice wonders, you wonder, could they possibly be gills? You kiss his neck and you can hear the babbling of the crowd, distant, water-bound, refracted.

The Women's Train

Who sees her first?

They argue about this later as they sit in the *kipyatilka*, huddled near the stove, drinking cups of the greenish-brown soup that they make from the leaves of cabbages.

Gakayev, the leader of the salvage party and head of the camp guards, claims that he was the one. *I saw her eye*, he says. *I saw it right through all the bodies. She blinked, you know, and that's how I saw her*. I lifted the others off of her, he says. It was easy, he says, like peeling a lemon. And he stops there, pleased with this sentence.

—My mother, she says, *mana máte.* They lift her and wrap her in a blanket. *Kur ir mana máte?*

—Speak Russian, someone says.

When they bring Mara back to the camp they carry her into the main guards' barracks. They put her near the stove like a cord of birchwood, and she wonders, for a moment, if she will be fed into the enormous, red-rimmed bellows. *A women's train,* she hears them saying in Russian, again and again, near and far, loud and soft. *For Elgen. No, no, a girl, only, just one.*

A buzzer sounds and they all stand immediately—all the men standing as one—and they prepare to leave for the meal tent.

—Dinner, Gakayev says, leaning over her with his pine-rot breath, hanging his rifle on a peg above her head. I will bring you something. Maybe a salmon heart, or a liver. You'd like that, wouldn't you—a nice salmon heart with some bright red caviar? Maybe a little vodka?

Behind him the men laugh, a chorus of appreciation. She looks up at him and she can feel the way the gun is swinging above her, moving just slightly on its peg, to the left and to the right.

—*Kur ir mana máte*? She asks him, her eyes caked closed with blood. He looks at her, pauses, nods. He laughs.

—Why? Are you going to go somewhere? It's twenty-below out there.

MARA IMAGINES how it was before the confusion, before all the stations and the crowded cattle cars and the cold. She remembers her mother, cooking dinner late on a Friday night, the kitchen thick with smoke and the reflections of its own windows. *Karbonade,* a pork chop, fried in butter on the stovetop. Wild mushrooms with vinegar and dill. Some bread, good bread, nothing like what they gave them in the trains. *Rudzumaize.* She imagines her father, peeling apples for dessert, peeling them and smoking his pipe, humming. Her father hums and listens to her mother talk. She tells him about a cousin who has landed in jail for growing flowers in the color of the Latvian flag.

GAKAYEV HAS TOLD HER where to go.

As the guards leave he tells her, laughing and strapping on his padded hat. The sound of his leaving lingers behind him, creates a presence in the absence of everything else. After some time, Mara stands, bumping her head against the gun. She sinks deeper into the blanket, covering all of her ragged and muddy, blood-perfumed dress. She opens the door and walks into the cold.

THREE BUILDINGS down the road. On the left. There will be a guard.

At the third building she sees him, waiting patiently in the snow, the snow dusted along his shoulders and his arms. He is leaning on a bicycle, leaning against it for support, almost as if he is too tired to stand. Mara has never felt anything like this, this cold that moves easily along your bones, that makes them shimmer with pain.

—*Sveiks,* she says, standing motionless in front of him. He doesn't answer. With an empty shudder, Mara realizes that the man is dead, that he is propped against the bicycle so that he doesn't collapse. Looking away from his figure, she opens the door and enters the morgue. *He looked so beautiful,* she thinks, *so pale.*

MARA LOOKS AT THEM, looks at the corpses, piled up along the walls all around the dissection table. It is a long room—perhaps twenty meters long—but narrow. The archway is stone—incongruous on a building otherwise fashioned from canvass and plywood—dark gray stones, stones divulged from somewhere within the permafrost.

There is almost no odor here, and almost no heating, and she wants to cry but she is unable, she is too cold. There will be no need for autopsy—the crash is evident in every head and neck that bulges, purple with the violence of its death. Resolutely, Mara moves from one pile to the next, pulling as best she can, tugging on hair and exposed skin and frozen fabric. Then, near the back of the room, she finds her—stacked atop two other women, lying on her back.

For a moment Mara forgets the temperature, forgets everything except the body. She is quiet; she cannot feel the pain in her arm. Then, without thinking, sure that she has finally come home after such a long journey, Mara clambers up the stack of bodies and lies on her mother's chest. She closes her eyes and she goes to sleep.

IT IS FOUR IN THE MORNING and they have been searching all night. Gakayev is tired: even the guards don't get enough food for this kind of exertion in the cold. He is smoking a cigarette near the doorway to the main building, talking with another guard—a gopher-faced little man who is new here but still calls Gakayev by his first name.

They are both wrapped in shawls—thick, grainy woolen shawls, bright red, effulgent in the rolling light of the single lamp on the lamppost. The cigarette burns close to his gloves—gloves that have both thumb and forefinger missing—and Gakayev cups the flame in the wool, brings air through it until the flame burns his fingers. This light is small in the dark, they are small figures in the larger darkness, a chain of illuminations from throat to mouth to the bulb above.

—Where, where could she possibly be?

—In a drift, Pavlo. She's dead. Let's go to sleep.

—We have to find her.

—Why? Who cares? The train wasn't coming here anyway. These are Balts—they've been coming through all week. They're headed north.

—But she was just a girl.

—And so? We cleared the tracks. That's all we had to do. This is *promot,* Pavlo, waste of camp resources. I don't want to be held responsible.

Gakayev looks at him. He sighs and nods his head. One girl can't matter, really, not when her mother was a political prisoner, an enemy of the state. With a nod he turns and begins to walk to the communications tent, where he will sound the bell to call off the search.

All night, for some reason, a memory has been troubling him. He has been remembering when he was a child, not far from here, only several hundred miles south, on the edge of the taiga, where the ground doesn't freeze all the way through. He has been remembering a walk he took, one day in the Spring, and how he uncovered, in the mud of an irrigation ditch, a nest of rats—a mother and her six young babies. The babies were newly-birthed, and the mother was exhausted; Gakayev scooped them up in his shirt almost without effort, carried them quickly back to his house.

—What are those? His mother asked him immediately, staring at his shirt, his new cotton shirt, which was soaked through and stained with water and afterbirth. She seized the bundle from him and unwrapped it on the kitchen table, drew in her breath and clicked her tongue against the roof of her mouth.

—You kill these things if you find them, Pavlo, she said. You don't bring them home.

And with one motion she bore them to the stove, dropped all seven rats in a kettle of boiling water.

And she was right, too, Gakayev is thinking, and then he is opening the tent flap, and suddenly there is another guard behind him, and everyone is shouting, and they are saying that they found the girl in the morgue, and that he needs to come, to come quickly, because he has to see what they've discovered.

Someone once said that in the marrow-bones of a grown man or woman, it is still possible to trace the outline of a child's bones, though the child's bones themselves have disappeared, have lengthened and thickened and grown.

Mara lies in the cold for a long time, moving through an uneasy sleep. She feels her mother's dead hands beneath her, feels them against the bones of her back, flat and soft despite their stiffness, still loving. She can feel herself dying, in a way, though this is entirely unremarkable, and she wonders about it for a moment, why it is taking so long. She listens to the sounds of the night around her—she can hear the sounds of it even though she is sleeping—and to her, it seems, there is a hum to it, a resonance and reverberation and tone. It is growing and rising from all around her, this sound that is somehow transformative, and then, it peaks, it begins to subside, to unravel, and then she thinks, once again, of the smell of frying pork chops.

There are nineteen camp guards following him. Each of them own a pair of government-issued HK-21 boots—broad boots with fur linings and dense soles made from new vulcanized rubber. No one speaks as they walk towards the morgue—they are all tired or afraid or unsure of what to say. Gakayev is their leader, they silently acknowledge this, and maybe he'll know what to do. The thirty-eight boots follow quickly through the frozen snow, popping through its surface with the precision and echo of a military parade.

When Gakayev reaches the tent he sees that the guard has been overturned. The front wheel of his bicycle is spinning, clicking gently as it spins, making a sound like rain. He pushes the body out of the way with his foot and stands at the open door. The light inside is dim; someone behind him shines a lantern into the darkness.

The bodies are still there. This cannot be questioned. All sixty-two bodies—the ones that could be salvaged and were not burnt at the site of the wreck. But those that he retrieved—that he himself supervised as they were loaded onto the transport-truck with its wheels like donuts—those were the bodies of women. These forms, here, these are all the corpses of children, of girls, small against their stone beds. How had they been transformed, altered, changed? These were the same women—there could be no doubt. But somehow they'd become younger. The years had disappeared, simple as breath through cold air.

Gakayev pauses for a moment, looks through the near-dark. He looks and looks and then, there, near the back of the room, he sees her, a quick shock—the girl who'd been brought to him earlier that day. There she is—he sees—and she is not moving. There is something so sad in all of this, something that is so sad that he almost wants to laugh, to pause a moment, laugh a little, and then order it all undone. To order enough food rations for the inmates, to requisition adequate fuel to heat the barracks, to lessen the work hours, hell, to open the gates to the whole camp, to say: *You are all free to make your way home. Here are a few rubles for the journey.*

Gakayev stands in the doorway and breathes the painfully cold air. He sighs. He turns his back to the room, turns to the expectant congregation of camp guards.

—Bury them, he says. Bury them now and quickly. Then let's see if we can't get some rest.

BUT GAKAYEV CAN'T SLEEP.

He can't stop thinking about the transformation, seemingly impossible, that occurred in the morgue. He paces from the door of his room to his cot, back and forth, again and again. He remembers his appointment to the camp, the punishment of an angry superior, disappointed by his love of vodka, perhaps. He remembers the first wave of inmates, sent east on the cattle cars without trial. He remembers the stench as they opened the cargo bay and found them all dead, overcome by the cold and starvation. A paperwork error, Gakayev later discovered, had sent the train to the wrong camp. Instead of processing the cars then, the guards had just parked them on the reserve tracks, and ignored the prisoners until they'd died.

What is this system, he thinks, one that takes thousands of civilians and ships them east without concern for their survival? How can all these people be guilty of capital crimes? These women—these girls, whatever they are—how could they all be traitors? How do their deaths glorify the Union? Once, Gakayev had been willing to do anything for the greater good of the state, but now—he's not so sure.

Tired, his eyes stinging, he slips on his heavy winter clothes and leaves the tent to smoke a cigarette in the winter air. Though it's really too cold to do this, he can't resist the impulse. He needs to get outside, to walk around the perimeter of the camp. He lights his cigarette in the shelter of the tent, then pulls aside the three canvas flaps, steps onto the crunchy frozen snow. The air mixes with the smoke and stings his lungs. Gakayev looks at the paste of stars in the sky. He can see Ursa Minor, Ursa Major, Orion. The stars are mute and watchful, distant. He wishes, briefly, that he could see himself from the perspective of this distant sky: Just as small and dull as he must truly be, his mouth lit only by a single, orange ember.

The Ping-Pong King of Kenosha, Wisconsin

At the age of ninety-two, my grandfather developed a passion for the game of ping-pong. At the age of ninety-three, he asked me to help him die.

Coming off a double shift at St. Catherine's on any given Thursday in August of 1999, I would have roughly ten messages on my answering machine. In the pale gray light of the early morning, I would sink into the leather sofa and listen, rubbing the weariness from my forehead, struggling to surface, however briefly, from the entombment of a 26-hour work day.

Message One:

My Mother, asking if I was still alive, hoping that I was still alive, not that she would know if I weren't.

Message Two:

The Gas Company, asking if I was still alive, and if I was, could I please mail them a check immediately.

Message Three:

My Grandfather, inviting me to the Melody Woods Retirement Community, to the First Annual Melody Woods Ping-Pong Invitational.

Message Four:

The Gas Company again, specifying that if I were deceased, this would not be sufficient excuse for failing to remit payment.

Messages Five Through Ten (Variable):

My Grandfather again, checking to see if I had received my invitation, and if I had, would I please RSVP, since seating was bound to be limited.

He was a beautiful old man, with blue eyes that seemed to darken every year, become more arcane and clever and insubstantial. His eyebrows were vast and white, and had thickened as his other hair had thinned. They formed a bright abutment at the top of his face. He bent over when he walked, almost so that he looked like a question mark, and his head was always dangling, bobbing a little as he smiled and talked. I would visit him sometimes at the home, negotiating the thinly-carpeted halls, trying to take the same furiously quick, tiny steps that he did. I always marveled at this staccato walk, whose steps, if elongated, would have easily equaled the pace of any marathon runner. Everywhere he went was a minor act of heroism—teetering to the algaeic pool to lay out in the sun, bobbing to the video room for Rented Movie Night, stuttering to the main hall to play a few songs on the piano.

Whenever I came to visit, my grandfather would introduce me to the women.

—Laura, this is my grandson, William Baldwin. William is studying to be a doctor.

—Why, Charles, were you this handsome when you were young? I'm so pleased to meet you, Mr. Baldwin. And a doctor, too? My grand-niece, I'm sure, would love you to death.

These conversations were almost always the same. Invariably, they brought murmurs of approval and ended with an invitation for him to play Yahtzee, or to have a cup of tea in the dining hall. My grandfather would give me a brief wink when accepting these invitations, his eyes glittering and distant. He would later confide that he used me to his advantage.

—A grandson who's a doctor? That always looks good to them. It helps me score, William, when they're tipsy after mahjong.

CONSIDER THIS: You're having lunch with your grandson at Andy's Restaurant on 63rd Street. You've ordered nothing, just a cup of black coffee. The pain in your stomach is worse than normal, feels as if a whole, hot fist is clenched in your gut. But you can't remember it, you can't remember what it is, and you have to focus to remember your grandson's name. Everything you say, everything he says, all the words have a second, subluminous halo. The coffee makes the pain worse, and suddenly you remember: Peptic ulcer, but then the pain rips upward through your chest and into your throat again, and you forget. These are the most stupid things you've ever seen—the motions of your hands through the air, the way the heat of the cup feels against your fingertips—and yet they bring you great sadness. Your grandson looks at you. *Why no food?* He asks, as always, and smiles a little.

—I don't need it, you say. At this age, you say, the body runs itself.

You're about to bluff, so you smile a little. You start talking about something else.

I'D ORDERED THE TUNA MELT and a glass of tomato juice. He'd

had nothing, just a cup of black coffee. That wasn't unusual, though. Often, when we'd go out like this, my grandfather would eat nothing. *I don't need it*, he would say. *At this age, the body runs itself.* The palace of taste, with all of its shimmering allure, was beyond the threshold of his needs. He had become an ascetic, in a way, and was living, as far as I could tell, on ping-pong alone.

—There's something beautiful about the game, he was telling me. Something so beautiful in the way the ball cuts down across the net, so fast. I'm so old, but still, I hit that ball and it just flies.

He was supposed to play, in four weeks, in the Second Annual Melody Woods Ping-Pong Invitational. He'd developed, over the course of a year, quite a league at Melody Woods. There was a rumor, he told me—a rumor that he himself had started—that a ping-pong *professional* was going to make an appearance. And he'd talked, he disclosed, to the Activities Supervisor about the possibility of videotaping the final match, videotaping it and airing it on public-access TV.

I had missed the First Annual Invitational, I told him, but I was planning on attending the second. *I was?* He asked. *Good. Good.* He wanted to make sure of that, he told me, because he wouldn't be there to supervise.

—What do you mean you won't be there to supervise? I asked.

THAT NIGHT, I walked down to the lighthouse that was on the rocky spit, the jut of land that bellied out from the shore a few miles from downtown.

Narcotic analgesics. The medication, I knew, would be easy enough to get. An opioid would slow his breathing—lower his tidal volume and his respiratory rate. His heart might stop just from this, and even if it didn't, there were other ways of ensuring that the process was painless.

I stood on the mounds of rocks that gave onto the broad pale body of Lake Michigan—the slick black rocks with their beds of molar crustaceans—and thought about my grandfather. Where would I look for an answer to this question, the one that I had been completely unprepared to answer? The alzheimer's was starting to debilitate him. Already, he had trouble recognizing his friends, he was always scared and sad and tired. He had talked with other doctors—though he never said which ones—and they had discussed his long-term prognosis. Yesterday, he said without breaking the seriousness of his voice, he had nearly fainted in the middle of a match, and had barely rallied, at the end, to win 22-20.

Hadn't I seen this very situation, I thought, in my biomedical ethics textbook? The earnest, young doctor-to-be, just about to finish his residency, is Confronted By a Difficult Decision. What does he do? Does he consult his family, his father and mother who live nearby in suburban Milwaukee, who call him constantly and have little on their minds? Or does he deny this well-reasoned, careful request, a request for which he was entirely unprepared, a request after which he could neither eat his food, nor drink his juice? Or does he procure the medication, take it to his grandfather, and sit quietly by his bedside? Does he ensure there is no autopsy? Does he gently supplant the on-call nursing-home doctor, sign away the body, and *then* call home? Does he tell his aging parents a simple story, one that they will readily believe, one that they will have no reason to doubt? These were the options, anyway, that I seemed to remember from the textbook.

The water tapped softly at the rocks, a cool dark sound.

Consider this: You love the game of ping-pong and you wonder if you will play it eternally, floating on the buttress of the clouds, angelic and elegant, wearing a nicely starched robe, a robe with a gossamer belt. You take the breath into your lungs—it is your last conscious breath—and you consider the inadequacy of it all, of all these human embattlements, against the siege of death. Then you look, you can still look though there will be no more breathing, and you see a photo, a bright gray image in a bright gray frame, on the wall near the window. It is your wife's autographed picture of Hosni Mubarak—a true rarity—and you'd forgotten that it was there, that you'd tacked the nail in yourself, six years earlier, when you'd moved here from your son's house. You smile, softly, remembering how excited she was when she received it in the mail, and you wonder what your grandson is thinking, sitting there beside the bed, in the still-breathing world. *Is it good weather today in Cairo?* You wonder, and then it all quietly separates, then the colors unravel simply, and you want to yawn but you can't feel your jaw.

The first round of the double-elimination tournament went quickly. An old man—Jake Saunders—swept easily through his opponents. He looked like the favorite; in four matches, he only surrendered two points, one of which came when he lost his glasses on a backhand. In the quarterfinals, though, he came up against some tough competition. Edna Alburas—a diminutive diabetic who played the game from her wheelchair—took him beyond the limit of 21. The score went back and forth as they traded points, each of them unwilling to concede, each of them stretching beyond the limits of their endurance. Finally, with it tied at 27, Saunders rattled off two quick aces. He was in the semi.

I had, of course, also been invited to compete in the Second Annual Melody Woods Ping-Pong Invitational. I lasted one game, a humiliating rout at the hands of an elderly woman named Vera. *She walks with a cane,* I considered. *She's nearly three times my age*, I thought, as I sent my last serve into the net.

They were good at ping-pong, these old people.

The first semifinal was a blowout. Jake Saunders, exhausted by the previous match, lost to the eventual champion, a palsied Southerner named Nathan Trebidault. When he finally did win the championship, Trebidault smiled at his opponent, gave a graceful bow to the vigorous applause of the audience. I was sitting in the third-row, surrounded on all sides by the elderly, and I stood to congratulate this man, to congratulate the champion, to shake his lightly trembling hand. Trebidault smiled as we touched. He didn't say anything. He averted his wet eyes and stared down at the carpet.

We had rehearsed this previously, with all of the players on the night before the tournament, the night after the one that my grandfather had chosen as his last. The eventual winner, it was decided, would come over and accept my salutations. He would take my hand as a symbolic remembrance, a commemoration, of all my grandfather's work. Without Charles, they'd all said, there would have been no Invitational.

No one, of course, suggested that I might win.

At the post-tournament reception, Jake Saunders came

slowly over, smiling sadly above his glass of Veuve Cliquot. He stood there for a moment, not speaking. The image of my grandfather dying—of him shuddering slightly and then easing back onto his bed, of his last breath, a deep and thick breath, a long and scudding sigh—the image would not stop raising itself onto the bright platform of my eyes.

—How long since he had his stroke? I asked, easing the silence and pointing across the room towards Trebidault. Seven, eight months?

—Nate? Saunders asked. Oh, a year, I think, since the last one. The recovery's been slower this time.

—He's had more than one, then? I had guessed perhaps...

I trailed off. *Perhaps,* I thought, *is a stupid and ridiculous word.* Saunders sipped at his champagne, swallowed, tightened his mouth at its edges.

—He's had four.

I nodded. Suddenly, I felt profoundly like an intruder, as if my presence here, as if the very fact of my youth, was some sort of an insult.

—I'm sorry. I didn't mean to, that is, I just meant that he makes a good champion, I concluded lamely.

Saunders raised his eyebrows at this, and tipped back his glass. He waited a moment more, then turned and walked back towards the wine steward. He spoke to me as he left, letting his words mingle with the noise of the reception.

—Have a good night, Doctor, he said. Try not to drink too much.

The Liars

It's after midnight when Wilbur wakes up. A burnished darkness hangs over everything, almost like a second skin. He's sitting immediately, the covers shuffling down his midriff towards the flat of the bed, and he can feel the cold on the tops of his feet where they've been exposed to the work of the air conditioner.

Why is he awake? He covers his legs and listens for some sound from his parents' room—their voices drawn into a tight song of argument—but he hears nothing. He looks outside. The March air shimmers in brown and purple arcs from the streetlamp to the window to the streetlamp. It's raining, just slightly, and the scent of it leaks through even the double-paned glass. *That must be it*, Wilbur thinks, then shakes his head slightly, realizing he's wrong. There's something else, too, something slightly foreign and cold.

This feeling broadens as he opens the door and walks into the hall. Something's unbalanced. He walks downstairs, takes a left into the living room. As he comes through the entrance to the kitchen he knows he's found it: the back door is open, wide-open, and the soft wind has spilled the wetness of the rain just over the threshold, onto the checkered tiles of the floor. Wilbur stands in the aperture, half-in, half-out.

The crickets are thick and monotonal, hypnotic. Wilbur

shakes his head. He's sure this has never happened before—a door opening itself in the middle of night. He looks closer. Someone has tracked leaves over the tiles. Wearing only his boxers, Wilbur breathes the steam of the suburban night, letting the humidity dampen the right side of his body. He can feel a pressure in the air, the pressure of New York, which he knows is just beyond those trees, its skyline bright and light-punctured and sprawling. After some time he startles—he's been asleep on his feet, swaying and precarious. Tired, certain he'll find nothing by lingering, he reaches for the doorknob, reaches out with the intention of pulling it shut. Then he stops. He shrugs and goes back to bed. He leaves the door open.

IN THE MORNING there's a strange woman at breakfast. She is sitting at the table reading the paper when Wilbur comes in, and he can only stare at her. She's wearing his mother's bathrobe. It's open at the front almost to the navel. From his vantage point, Wilbur can see the pale curvature of her breast as it tucks beneath a fold of the thick cotton. It is, he observes quickly, the color of toast, unbuttered toast, toast just like the two slices that are quartered, so neatly quartered, on the kitchen table. The woman looks up from the front page and smiles at him. His father, Wilbur notices belatedly, is standing at the stove, hunched over a pan that is full of a brown, charred-smelling mixture.

—Good morning, Wilbur. This is my mistress, Candy Johnson. Candy, Wilbur. Wilbur, Candy. Would anyone like eggs?

Now Wilbur notices his mother, sobbing wildly in the living room. His mother, whose thick black hair he can see over the edge of the sofa, sobbing and screaming, her voice a ragged threnody of grief. He immediately moves towards the living room but stops—frozen by a gesture from his father, who has, Wilbur now sees, a deep bleeding gash above his left eye. His dad is shaking his head, bunching the skin of his eyebrows together, which makes his face look like a map—marked and carved with red and black lines. His eyes are funny, kind of like a glazed donut, and he looks just above Wilbur, he doesn't look into Wilbur's eyes.

On the floor in the passageway between the two rooms there is a shattered vase, and Wilbur thinks: *How did I miss this? Was I in the shower?*

—Maybe no eggs, Will?

—Dad?

—Why don't you just run along to the bus?

His father is pushing him now, frying pan in one hand, towards the opening door. Charred egg is falling on the floor.

—Dad, it's July. I don't have school.

—That's good. Now, see you later. Love you.

The door closes, and Wilbur is left standing on the stoop, wearing little more than last night—only boxers and a t-shirt. He turns and tries to peer through the window. *You asshole,* he hears his mother scream, and then he hears the radio in the kitchen, suddenly turned on as loud as it can go, and it's playing a waltz, and he thinks he can just make out—between the folds of the window-treatment on the kitchen door—two figures waltzing slowly, languorously, to the music.

It's summer, so Wilbur and his friends play basketball. They're not good—constant traveling, wildly missed shots, flagrant and desperate fouls—and Wilbur feels like a circus act, an unskilled pretender trapped in an inelegant game. They scuffle and shoot and flail and then lose interest. They sag along the fence, sitting on the pebbly asphalt. The ball scrabbles listlessly away.

—It's hot, someone says.

Wilbur agrees. He lies down on the court, where there's a little shade from a nearby building. He can feel the sear of the sun on the raised planes of his face.

—Did you ever wonder, he asks no one in particular, if you'd sink into this stuff if you slept here long enough?

No one answers. Then someone says, the sun's not up enough hours for that, and then someone else disagrees, and then it's quiet again. Wilbur imagines floating up from the blacktop and rising into the sun. It would burn. Or maybe it wouldn't—maybe it would be too fast to burn. Who could say? No one had ever done it, so no one knew for sure. It was an unknown. He looked to his left. His friends had arranged themselves in a row—five of them—all of them quiet, all lying near the baseline.

STILL-LIFE with Flushing, New York.

Elder Avenue, and a respectable duplex condominium. His mother buys it with the divorce settlement. It has aluminum siding. Often, at night, Wilbur stands outside and leans against the walls, watching the traffic whisk by against the backdrop of the darkened park. *This is aluminum*, he observes. *I sleep encased in aluminum.* His mother has started on the pills, of course, and she lines them up carefully on her dinner plate, invariably near the meat, a pharmeceutical rainbow. Ghost pink Paxil, pale green Remeron, robin's egg Xanax—why are they all pastel?

His father, however, moves with Candy to Alphabet City, where they share a roach-infested studio. There are no blinds or curtains on the windows. There is no furniture, in fact, except for two mattresses and a kitchen table. It's a nice kitchen table, though—a fine formica top, a tasteful green and yellow checkerboard design—and Wilbur's father spends a good deal of time polishing it, running a damp washcloth over its surface in broad, loping circles. His father has forgone pills and skipped straight to recreational drugs. He calls marijuana by its antique name—*grass*—and Wilbur feels a rush of kitsch whenever he spends the night downtown. *Would you like some grass, Wilbur?* His dad says. *How's college?* Wilbur smiles and accepts and lights it and inhales. I haven't applied, dad, he reminds him. I'm too busy with your problems.

WILBUR IS SEVENTEEN. He often thinks about this fact when he is lying on his mattress, closing his eyes tightly and trying to ignore the noises coming from his father's side of the room. *I'm seventeen,* he thinks, and stops at that. The numbers hang there, suspended and slightly luminous, backlit. And what a funny ceiling, he continues, it's colored like the courts at Wimbledon—precise green, green the color of lush grass, a green ceiling, who knew? He imagines a tennis game moving across it, the serves and volleys and incessant pounding rallies.

At the custody hearing in the judge's chambers, the attorneys for his parents sit in stuffed leather chairs and chat pleasantly about the Yankees. Wilbur can see his dad—who has taken a seat near the door—winking at him and nodding slowly.

—Strippers, he mouths, and then smiles broadly, just so his son will be sure to understand.

AND—exactly as advertised—here come the strippers, a thunderous burlesque, swollen and colorful and drunk.

Candy lasts eight weeks. She keeps her clothes in a cardboard box near the door, and her hygiene products clutter like fungus in the bathroom. One day, though, she's gone—all evidence of her presence disappears—and there's a replacement, too, a brunette named Christmas. She's pregnant when she moves in, and just beginning to show. She smokes constantly, too, Kool Menthols, and Wilbur wonders if the baby will be born addicted to nicotine. Or with black lungs. Christmas wears her hair in pigtails and drinks whole pots of coffee. Her teeth are stained with brown half-moons.

As far as Wilbur can tell, his father has forgone his job at Xerox in order to spend the remainder of his life in strip clubs—just hanging around and running occasional errands for the women. Wilbur comes along to one of them—The Crystal Palace, in downtown Queens—and he is amazed: It is a moveable feast of bodies, a banquet of naked breasts and stomachs and thighs. A few of the women know his father by name. Wilbur tries not to look at them, even when they're onstage.

He and his father visit the dressing room late that night, and his dad seems to shrink, to become smaller and more stooped and entirely sleazy. His moustache grows. His eyebrows sprout and thicken and gray. He is in every respect a pervert, a dirty old man who happens, by some unfortunate coincidence, to carry half of Wilbur's genetic code. *Hey, Mid-Life,* one of the women calls, beckoning with a red acrylic-tipped hand, and his dad shuffles over, walking like Charlie Chaplin.

WILBUR STAYS WITH HIS FATHER on the weekends and his mother during the week. His mom cooks meatloaf in two-pound tins, and each night she gnaws at the edges of a piece, managing a few mouthfuls, washing it all down with Maker's Mark or Five O'Clock Vodka. The only time she mentions Wilbur's father is on a Wednesday night near Thanksgiving. The two of them are eating dinner in front of the living room TV—mother and son, perched in front of a network rerun, the reception grainy and imprecise—and it is a commercial, a local commercial, for a department store, the After-Thanksgiving Sale. His mother has been half-asleep—they've both been watching in silence—when suddenly she sits upright on the sofa and points at the television.

—That tie! Your dad has that very tie! I gave it to him. And now it's half-off.

Wilbur stares at his mom, his mouth slightly open, the breath moving gradually in and out of his lungs. She's quiet for a moment, the commercial ends, and she sinks back into the upholstery.

—Damn it, she adds, and then she half-closes her eyes.

Wilbur moves a bite of the meatloaf from his plate to his lips. It's shiny, he notices. It has a certain plastic look about it, almost as if it's not real food at all.

ON CHRISTMAS MORNING, the twenty-fifth of December, Christmas the Stripper has been up all night, somewhere other than the apartment, and she blasts through the door just after sunrise, staggering and thick with the scent of alcohol. There's only one room to the studio, so both Wilbur and his father wake up. Wilbur's dad goes back to sleep—he doesn't ask much of these women, anyway—and Wilbur is left alone with Christmas, who stumbles into the kitchen and pours herself some tap water. She is singing a melody over and over—it sounds a little like

Happy Birthday To Me—and she takes one sip and drops the glass. Somehow it doesn't shatter. It bounces instead, and rolls loudly across the linoleum floor.

Christmas walks over and sits down. She stops singing and turns to Wilbur, who is protectively clutching his sleeping bag to his chest. She smiles.

—It's like, my second birthday, because it's my name and it's also totally Christmas.

She fumbles in her purse and takes out a little oval mirror. She has a nearly-empty, ochre-colored, screw-top vial, and she shakes it, and after some time a little white cube tumbles from its bottom. She has a razor, too, Wilbur sees, and he watches her crush the cocaine with the edge of the blade, gently, as if she is feeding a baby off of the knife. Christmas concentrates on this process, diligently forming two small lines in the center of the glass. Then she fishes in her handbag for something else. She pulls out a stack of folded money, leafs through it and selects what looks, to Wilbur, like a hundred.

—It feels better with a bigger bill, she says. You want a line?

He coughs, and runs his hand through his hair.

—No thanks, he says. Then he cringes. Not right now, anyway, he adds, to give it just the right tone.

Christmas shrugs and leans into the mirror. She inhales, throws her head back. She massages her neck with both of her palms.

—Half a gram for me, she says towards the ceiling. And half a gram for baby.

Then she looks at Wilbur and she smiles again and, for the first time, he notices that one of her incisors is missing.

His mother is losing her mind. He comes home one January afternoon and finds her wearing a lavender ball gown, an oversized top hat and tails, and rhinestone-crusted heels. She is chain smoking too, now—Kool Menthols, just like Christmas. *Ah, Wilbur,* she says one evening, while the two of them are doing dishes. *I am the Queen Top Hat. I float like an enormous balloon. I can sing the wind with these two fingers.*

—What the hell are you talking about, Mom?

—Nothing, honey. Go do your homework.

—You don't even smoke.

She shakes her head.

—Poor boy. I am the Queen Top Hat, and he doesn't even know it.

She insists on wearing the costume to dinner. It's the same meatloaf, and Wilbur wonders: Who do I call to have her committed? Is this even the right thing to do? Doesn't everyone have eccentricities? Some people collect model trains, some people tae-bo. His mother wears formal gowns to dinner, and talks in gibberish.

—*Du pain, s'il vous plait?*

Or make that French. Wilbur sighs.

—You want the bread? He asks, and she nods. He passes her the bowl and thinks: Other kids must have normal families, right? Every family—even the ones in the middle of a divorce—every family can't be like this.

One night later that month, Wilbur wakes up to Christmas sliding into his sleeping bag. She is naked, and he can feel the bulge of her stomach, tight but watery, between his legs. *What is she doing?* He thinks. *Can pregnant women do this?*

—But my dad—

—Shut up. He's a heavy sleeper.

She runs her hand aggressively along his chest, grabbing the waistband of his boxers with a flourish of her nails. She is greedy—he can tell this about her—and he whimpers a little as she kisses his neck. It's not that he doesn't want to, it's just—

—First time? She says.

Oh, yes, he thinks. *Oh, God yes. But who would believe me?*

—Not at all, he whispers.

AND THEN, just before Valentine's Day, Christmas disappears. She leaves all of her suitcases and her belongings. After a few days, Wilbur and his father are interviewed by the police. The officers are bored—one of them is folding a credit card receipt into an origami crane.

—Was Christmas her given name, Mr. Ellison?

—You know, Wilbur's father says, I'm not really sure.

The two cops exchange looks. The one who was talking snaps his notebook shut.

—We'll let you know, he says, if she turns up.

He might as well say: We'll never find her. Happens all the time. She's probably at some morgue in the suburbs, another Jane Doe, anonymous.

After they leave, Wilbur's dad sits on the floor beneath the little table. He looks ridiculous there, like some sort of over-sized doll, and he seems to be concentrating on the ground, which is covered in a ratty, tan carpet. His hand leans on the table and—in the pale light off the checkerboard design—Wilbur sees that his father's veins are vericose, that his skin is mottled and marked with age.

In cities, together and Apart

When killing a pig, Frank's cousin had said, *you never let its legs hit the ground. If they do, it might bolt, and the blood gets everywhere then.*

When loving an alcoholic, Shelby often told herself, the important question is not: Why? Instead, the important question is: What color of rhododendron would work best in this flowerbed, this one here, the one near the driveway? Would a yellow show up against the concrete? Or would it be washed out, faded by the gray? Maybe red? Something more vibrant? Something maroon? And should I trim these hedges? Are they too unruly? The lawn could use a little fertilizer, don't you think?

within a few seconds, the pig was dead. Its legs buckled and it made a pregnant small sound as it toppled. There was so much blood though, and it got on the edges of his shoes.

Frank and his cousin carried the pig across the field and back to the house. Recently privatized, the farm seemed vacant, desolate, ghostly. The previous tenants—fifteen of them, and mostly Russian—had gone. Only Frank's cousin lived there, now. He had populated the *kolhoze* with his small family, a new pioneer.

Once they neared the house, Frank handed the animal to his cousin. The other man took it, still dripping, towards the kitchen door.

—We don't drain blood when we eat, he said in English, stressing the second *we* with a roughness in his voice, with a certain, precise disdain. He stood on the threshold of the house, one hand on the doorknob.

Frank blanched but said nothing. His cousin disappeared into the kitchen. Frank stayed outside and lit a cigarette.

The fresh-cut flowers had beads of water on their skin. Six tulips—three of them open into a thick violet color, three curled into pale green layerings, shaped like the hands of infants.

Imperial, Shelby thought as she drove through the rain towards Seattle-Tacoma International, *that's probably its informal name. Imperial Treasure, or Purple Regent, or something just as hideous.* It's a shame, she thought, that English gardeners gave such awful names to flowers, when their origins, their etymologies, were so beautiful.

Tulip, from the Turkish *türbend*, because the early Europeans thought they resembled turbans.

Or irises, *iridos,* iridescent, the Greek goddess of the rainbow.

The rain skittered across the window of the blue Volvo stationwagon.

THE HAND that had held the knife wouldn't stop shaking. In the taxi—heading from his cousin's farm to the hotel in downtown Riga—Frank massaged his palm, rested his head against the window. *What could stop it from shaking? What if this was permanent?*

—I'm a marked man, he told the taxi driver, the alcohol spiraling through his head, back to front. They'd had a banquet and he'd drunk a bottle of vodka, himself. He scratched his head.

—You know, last year, ninety-six of us were killed, worldwide. Being a freelance journalist is worse than being a soldier.

The driver said nothing. And so Frank leaned back against the window. He couldn't stop thinking about the pig. It had been so large. About the size of a Lazy-Boy. Bright pink, but with a thin, surprising coat of hair. He hadn't known that the skin of pigs was coarse.

Frank had sucked in his breath, his own skin was pale as a crepe, waxen and pinched along the bones of his face. *Don't let its feet hit the ground. Don't let it bolt.* He'd held the rough wooden handle of his cousin's hunting knife at the edge of the animal's throat. He'd looked intently for the curvature where he expected to find the artery, and thought: *It has more hair than me.* The animal's eyes had swiveled in their sockets. The blade had scalloped through the flesh, softly at first, and the pig had whined and tried to bite its own neck. Frank had severed the vocal chords quickly, shocked by the blood. Bile was in his throat, and the pig blood was spattered on his light blue, cotton sleeves. The blood was part of the pig, and then it was a part of his clothes, of the ground, of the sour, late November air.

And then they were at the hotel, surprisingly fast, and Frank was struggling to find the words.

—This is fine, he said. This is fine, right here.

The little green Lada pulled to a stop outside the Hotel Latvia.

Frank fished for the money in his pocket, looked through the little window. A prostitute was leaning against a patch of graffiti on the hotel wall. *Shit on the floor*, it advised in Latvian. *Ruin it for the rest of them.*

Driving home that morning from the grocery store, thick, dark smoke had begun to pour from beneath the hood of her car. Shelby had killed the engine, coaxed the car over to the side of the Interstate. What could she do? She staggered from the car, propped open the hood, stared into the hot smoke. There was nothing she could do. It was raining then, and everything was a rush of motion and pure color and Shelby just turned towards the traffic and stood there, watching the magnificent roar, helpless. It was a trout colored sky.

—Two lati, sir.

—Here's five, keep the change.

The driver sighed as Frank clambered out of the little green Lada. *These Americans,* he thought, *these stupid Americans.* The three *latu* tip was almost two days' salary.

Vile love.

Shelby screamed and leapt from her seat and actually hit her head, lightly, on the padded ceiling. It was Danny, the valet at her health club. She'd known him for years—he was maybe twenty, twenty-one—but she'd never seen him outside the context of the parking lot, of the key ring and the three dollar tip, the opened door, heavy and swinging on its pendulum hinge. He smiled.

—Hello, ma'am.

Shelby brushed her hair from her eyes.

—Danny? Where'd you come from?

—I recognized your car on the side of the road. I stopped as soon as I could.

He motioned up the highway. His truck was just visible, a small red smear.

—You recognized my car?

He smiled again.

—1987 Volvo GS, Turbo. 4-door sedan, vapor blue, dual-exhaust, custom bumper, chrome strip and black plastic composite. Licence # HGC-192. Tags, January 2000. Dent, right side, near fender—

—Danny?

—Low-speed impact, less than five miles-per-hour. Scratch near keyhole, probably from the key, minor accumulation of rust. University of Washington parking permit, 1989-90 academic year. Bose speakers. One copy of Glamour magazine, cover torn, date illegible.

He seemed to be finished. Her mouth hung open.

—Your car.

FRANK WALKED from the taxi towards the front entrance to the hotel. He smiled at the prostitute as he passed her and then, halfway into the lobby, he heard her laughter—a long low sound like a horse. He went back outside.

—What? He asked. What did I do?

—Nothing, nothing. *Bet tu edi gan so vakar, ko?* But you ate a big meal tonight, I'll bet.

He nodded. He looked at her leg, long and thick, cased in torn nylon.

—Yes, ma'am, he said, in English. And then: *Edu gan.* Yes, I did, absolutely.

—*Un bija trekns?* And it was greasy?

—Greasy and delicious.

And then she was laughing, and she had him by the back of his shirt, and then she was pressing him against the wall, holding his head straight with her hands.

—And you had a few drinks tonight, too?

He looked at her because he had no choice. His head was pinned and would not move. Who was this woman? A hooker, sure, and this, this wall behind him—this was his hotel. But beyond this, Frank had no ability to tell. He couldn't remember anything. And what was there to remember, anyway, besides the bottle of vodka, the sweet scent of juniper when he'd unscrewed its top?

The woman dropped one hand and slipped it, ornately, along the bulging curvature of Frank's side. She smiled, then, her mouth opening, her lower jaw moving forward. Her tongue was tensed on the edge of her lips. And then, not knowing why, he reached out his mouth and traced the abrasions of her lips, brushed against the serrated, chapped skin. He counted the gold caps on the ends of her teeth. He counted, as an infant does, with his tongue.

DANNY WAS A PIMPLY, sickly-thin, high-school dropout who, rumor at the club had it, lived with his drunk mother and their twenty cats. He had a wispy moustache, one that aspired to be a goatee, and luminous dark brown eyes, irises that rose in a single block of color, nearly as dark as the emptiness of their pupils. His odor, Shelby discovered as she rode in the cab of his truck, was quite overwhelming, part mildew and part Clearasil. His clothes needed to be washed, his face needed to be washed, his nails were greasy—slick with a shiny substance.

But he'd called her ma'am, and this, to be quite honest, turned her on. And they drove quietly away from her car—north on the highway to Aurora Boulevard, Exit 169, and an endless succession of strip malls. The little truck sputtered up to a row of rundown, eighty-year-old, wood-frame homes—five bedroom houses with chapped paint and sagging porches—all of them squeezed between Bill Pierre Ford and the drive-in Burgermaster. The front door jammed, and Danny threw his shoulder into it, and they entered the dark house close together.

—The phone's in here, Danny said, and brought her an old rotary.

Oddly, he didn't move to turn on any lights, and the air was filled with a rotting, sweet perfume. Shelby called AAA; Danny rummaged through the kitchen, clattering through the cupboards and the refrigerator. She hung up; he reappeared with one can of Coors Light. He sipped at it and loomed in the doorway, strange and gangly and colored like spackle. He wouldn't say anything—there was a long, silent pause—and Shelby wondered if he would ever talk, if she could just walk past him silently, walk through the front door and catch a bus home, if she could disappear without thanking him, without speaking at all. Would he wave goodbye? And did he intend to drink that whole beer himself?

—A tow truck's coming, she said. Thirty minutes. It'll meet me here.

Danny didn't seem to notice that she was saying anything. Shelby started getting nervous.

—How old are you, anyway?

He smiled, then, a crooked smile that stuck to one of his front teeth. He cleared his throat.

—Mom's not here, he said. You want to see something special?

When killing a pig, Frank's cousin said, *the important thing to remember is not to drop the knife. And take these.* He gave Frank a handful of trout lily, their broad leaves covered with red blotches. Rub these on your hands.

Frank looked at his cousin.

—Flowers?

His cousin coughed.

—I don't know. My wife, she tells me these things.

Frank looked down at the two blooms, their stems crossed above his palms.

Shelby loved these flowers. But what did she call them? Didn't she call them something else?

Dogtooth violet? Was that right? Frank remembered always wanting to eat the flowers in his mother's garden, remembered yearning to fill his mouth with them, to roll their pulp over his tongue, to chew.

Later, when Shelby had closed the door to her own house behind her, when she had turned the deadbolt and stood with her back to the door, breathing deeply, shaking a little, her throat dry and in need of a drink, when she'd showered and shaved her legs and boiled some pasta and listened to Frank's message on the machine, only then was she able to forget, for a moment, the experience of Danny's basement.

Nineteen stairs, and that scent—the sweet rot that she'd smelled as soon as they'd come through the door—that odor had intensified. Danny had flipped on the light and revealed what looked to her like a normal basement: silvery cobwebs on the ceiling, an aging washer and dryer, some cardboard boxes and a few wooden crates. But then he'd crossed the room and approached a second door, had pulled a key from his pocket and moved his hand towards the silvery padlock.

You assumed a shared experience with the people around you.

This was Danny's garbage room, and it was overflowing with trash, with a wet, decaying layer of food products and dirty towels, with rotten fruits and vegetables and various, incongruous pieces of broken furniture. The trash rose from the floor to near waist level, and it stretched from the door to the wall, a high-stacked, fetid mess. There were flies, a swirl of black flies with shiny metallic wings, and the scent was something like vomit.

Once, when she was a child, Shelby had visited the City of Seattle Landfill with her mother. It was an overcast day and the seagulls were blurs of white against the sky. Shelby was amazed; the discarded items seemed almost perverse, damp with the hands of the people who'd dumped them, thick with the memories of possession and the surplus value of their love. Here, Danny had the things that people had spat on, had partially chewed, had sweated into and sat on and loved, however briefly. And they stank.

She was disgusted.

—Sometimes I take out the old stuff, he said, and I bring in new stuff. So do you want to kiss me, or what?

On the flight home he was in business class.

—Would you like a drink, sir? It was the steward, asking him before the plane began its taxi.

—A drink?

The English was strange, a foreign sound. He was shuttling between two cultures, two languages, two lives. Between his wife, whom he loved, and this second, more brutal kind of living. He stared at the steward, unable to form a reply.

—I'm sorry, sir. I'll just come back.

When the steward left, Frank hid his face with the sleeve of his suit and began to cry.

Waiting, standing at the airport gate, Shelby looked at the tulips.

And yes, actually, she had wanted to kiss him, to make love with him in the trash, the brown water rising over her hands, his figure behind her, his bony, slick hands on the sides of her hips. That stench filling her nostrils, billowing and rotten and sharp.

But Frank. Frank would bring back gifts from Latvia, Shelby knew—he always did. There would be salmon roe caviar, cheap novelty cigarettes, bottles of black balsam liquor. He would leave and return with spoils, looting the duty free stores, a modern Viking with a Gold Card. She could hear his thick voice, now. She had remembered, standing there in the basement, his lazy businessman's laugh. *Thank you, Danny,* she'd said, *but I don't think I can.*

Waiting, standing at the gate, Shelby had been fascinated by the color of the late evening sky. The clouds had been partial, and some of the last sunlight had managed to scissor its way through, seaming the sky with faint lines of orange and blue. Shelby had imagined ascending into those clouds, rising into them in the body of a plane, and had imagined how their light would envelop her, saturate her vision. I'd be blinded, sure, Shelby had thought, but at least I'd be blinded by color.

The Emigrant

Samir is a juggler of frogs.

Living animals with raw, green skin—he grabs them by their bellies and spins them in an arc through the air. They are an amphibian chorus. They announce him as he makes his way through the streets of Cairo—offering his frogs from the Royal Palace to the Qasr El Nil barracks. He walks all day, and his feet and legs ache with a coating of fine taupe dust.

It's early evening. The August air is full of the stench of the city—exhaust from the military vehicles, decomposing trash, a faint odor of sewage. Samir stops to rest near the looping barbed wire of the barracks fence, placing his hands on his knees and breathing deeply. The skin beneath his galabiyya rises into sweat. The frogs are loud in their canvass sack, and the mud and water he gives them so that they'll stay alive is leaking onto the ground.

Here, near the ornate walls of the Qasr El Nil, Samir can hear the sounds of the base. In the main yard they are training at arms and artillery fire. Samir listens to the measured cadence of the instructor, the periodic clatter of the guns. Rumor says the Americans are coming soon, and that they'll share this base with the British. He believes this rumor, simply because he's sure it's his destiny: he's headed to Hollywood, to become a movie star, known around the world, just like Cary Grant and Clark Gable. He'll be atop the billing before long, with his new American name:

Nicholas Muscular

in

Love and Crime and War
and Heroic Brave Duels At Sea

Also starring:

GRETA GARBO *and*
HEDDY LAMAR *and*
KATHARINE HEPBURN *and*
CLAUDETTE COLBERT *and*
MARILYN MONROE

He has invented his name since everyone, he understands, invents a new name in Hollywood. And the title of the film, he figures, is open for discussion. The number of starlets, he also realizes, might have to be increased.

He's been practicing his English on the weekends at the cinema, paying for one movie but staying all day. Some mornings he rehearses lines on the street. He becomes the untouchable Capone, an outlaw, running from the police but still the hero. —You ain't gonna catch me coppah, see. You ain't gonna take me alive—Samir says, hoping that his lips can frame the perfect Chicago sneer.

Samir tries to imagine life in the army, or in Hollywood, or anywhere else but here, here where he has to carry around the frogs, negotiating the intricacies of their tumbling, squirming bodies. Here, where his only money is the occasional twenty piaster coin that a soldier might throw from behind the fence. These coins are broad silver discs. Samir remembers to look closely at the coins as they wobble towards him. He knows that you can see your future in the path of a coin through the air, in the glimmering residue it leaves as it flies. He catches them and presses them into his palms, imprinting their Arabic inscription on his skin.

And the soldiers are the only ones who'll pay, lately, and the British are the most generous among them. Samir's mother says that this is their colonial guilt. She says it with a sneer, and though Samir doesn't really understand what she means, he nods as if he agrees. He does know, though, that there have been numerous comings and goings at the barracks—thousands of scrubbed, pink faces shuttling through on their way to Mersa Matruh. He hears them name this place with a certain, grim caution. There is a man there, they say, who lives in the desert with a fox. Though Samir understands little of it all, he gathers that the soldiers hate this man very much.

The heat of the day wraps Samir in its cocoon. This is the best time to stand at the fence, just as the day's exercises conclude and the soldiers return to prepare for their evening meal. Samir sees the first of them coming in across the field. He takes three frogs from the sack and tosses them, one at a time, into the air.

—Hey, Wally. He's here again. It's the frog juggler.

The voice floats towards him and soon he can see, in his peripheral vision, the faces of several soldiers, growing larger and approaching him. At home, Samir has a book about vaudeville, written in Paris by the magician Robert-Houdin, and he imagines that he would have been the second-to-last act on the billing: Nicholas Muscular and His Fabulous Flying Frogs. And the men and women would cheer as he tossed them higher and higher, adding frog after frog until his hands were conducting a constant, green blur.

—Can you look up, boy? How do you do it?

—He don't speak English, Wally. None of 'em speak English.

And it is a good audience, despite this: there are at least four soldiers watching from the other side of the fence. One of them is bound to have a coin of some sort for the street performer. Samir fills with the joy of performance, and stretches his hands further apart, broadening the path of the frogs through the evening sky. The poor creatures are croaking madly, bewildered and trying to get a foothold on the air. Samir is laughing, and then he starts to hear a whistle, faint at first but quickly getting louder. Someone is yelling, then, *Lookout!* And there is a puff, like the first exhalation of a steam engine, followed immediately by a pulse of heat, and then the ground seems to open and roar and swallow him, and his leg sears and his ears feel like they are about to burst. Samir opens his mouth as he tumbles through the explosion, he opens his mouth because he can't manage to open his eyes, and he finds only dirt, not air, foul-tasting dirt that's grainy and thick across his tongue.

Each morning, Samir's mother, Fatima Habib, awakes before dawn, stretching her limbs in the darkness that's like a musk on their bodies. During the day, she works for a local dukkan, selling live chickens from a basket on her head. She keeps them in the courtyard while she sleeps, locked in a windowless pen.

Each morning, Fatima steps in turn over her husband and her son, waking them up with the sound of her footfall. This is Samir's first sensual memory, the bottoms of his mother's feet, swooping over him in the dim light. Samir's father is blind.

Yusef Habib works as a French tutor to the cousins of the King. He hobbles through the streets every day behind the white donkey of the fruit salesman. The beast stumbles steadily ahead through city's háras, carrying two wicker satchels full of fruit. For one piaster per week, Yusef holds onto its tail and is led to work. This is, he figures, a form of public transportation. Soon, Samir will be old enough to guide his father. But for now, Yusef considers himself lucky to walk behind the donkey, though the stench is tremendous, and the laughter is occasionally quite fierce.

—My life is a litany of miracles.— He tells his son. They have been saying rosaries for the trip to America. Gathered at night in their single room, the family recites the litany of prayer. *Sacré coeur de Jesus, j'ai confiance en vous.* They repeat over and over, kneeling on the cold floor, their knees aching with the work of it. It's strange, Yusef knows, to be praying for something so foreign and so vast, such a dislocation and destruction of everything he knows. His son will be lost, he fears, and he and his wife—what can they possibly hope to do in America? But they are Coptic Christians, and the song of the city barely rustles with their chants. Yusef also knows that his odds aren't good. The United States, people say, will be closing its borders to Egyptians soon after the war.

—Why don't we just build our own boat and go?— Samir asks, late one night, looking through the window. —You could do it, with mother. I could help get the wood.

—And once it's built? We'll row to America? Across the Atlantic?

—Sure, papa, why not? How long could it take? One week,

two weeks? You can row. You're strong.

Yusef laughs and reaches out for his son's bed in the darkness. He can't find it, and he thinks that the boy must be curled near the window, looking up through the coal haze at the moon. Yusef remembers the moon quite clearly, from when he was Samir's age, and the memory of it floats brightly in front of him, large and distended, a luminous blue that moves him gradually into sleep.

EACH MORNING, Yusef kisses Fatima on the lips. *My neck aches,* she often says. And so he puts his hands on her shoulders, feels along her backbone. Yusef often imagines the vertebrae, with their steady disclosures of pain, lying in a row beneath her skin. He massages her neck. Outside, the fruit vendor calls.

By this point, the boy will have been ready for almost an hour. He will have had his breakfast, coffee and milk together in a mug, and a disc of aysh, the hard bread that softens in the coffee. He will have checked on the frogs—kept just inside the door in a bucket—and found, perhaps, that one of them died overnight. He will have thrown its body through the hallway window and out onto the street, no ceremony. He will have rubbed the other frogs with a cool mud, and fed them a handful of insects from a sealed jar that he keeps under the sink. He will have replaced the dead frog with a new one from the pond that sits a hundred meters from his family's apartment building—not uncommon in this part of the city—dank and undrained and malarial.

—Are you ready, Samir?

—Always ready, yes, always ready.—

His own litany, and he will take the older man's hand and

lead him through the doorway.

This morning, the city was an immediate assault, rising and spinning into sight and sound and scent. There was the feel of the day, a hot Cairo six a.m., miserable month of August, pungent and dusty and florid. Today, however, there was also the scent of roasting meat, a rarity. One of their neighbors, Yusef told his son, was grilling a goat.

War had quieted Cairo, though, had tempered the rush of its traffic. Gasoline rationing meant that only essential vehicles, mostly driven by British officials, hurried along the narrow streets. There were fewer cars because of this, but the roads weren't much safer. The British drove with displaced anger, careening from left lane to right lane, ignoring the street signs and menacing pedestrians. And, because the auto mechanics tended to be revolutionaries, their cars were unreliable. Lubricate the valves with sawdust, the story went, loosen the bolts holding the engine in place, overcharge for parts and labor: Nasser will thank you when the British diplomats drive to their deaths. Maybe you'll even get a government position.

The fruit vendor, though, greeted Samir and Yusef with a silent nod. He avoided looking at them, even when they paid him, and silently put the donkey's tail in the palm of Yusef's hand. It brayed when he did this, and the vendor slapped it with his whip, saying something under his breath. With a jolt, the beast started moving forward. Its back curved beneath the weight of the fruit baskets that hung, pendular, on either side of its frame.

The little convoy started down Sherif, their alley, and turned onto Talaat Harb, then eastward on Sabri Abu-Alam and out of the Popular Quarters. The vendor began shouting as soon as he reached the thoroughfare, his voice rising and falling, his sales pitch becoming a seductive song.

—Honey, here! Such sweet oranges! Honey-sweet oranges!

Almost immediately, a crowd of boys foamed up around them, loud and chattering, a swirling mass of brown and black hair. They were after the overripe fruit that the vendor could no longer sell and sometimes gave them: the sugary bananas, browned beyond recognition, the mangos gone patchy with sweetness, the purple-black figs that were both grainy and soft and shaped, everyone said, like the tears of elephants. But they were also after the blind man, Samir's father, who appeared every morning, holding the tail of a donkey. *Baby donkey shit, baby donkey shit,* they yelled, *where are you going today, baby donkey shit?* And though he recognized some of the boys, Samir could say nothing that wouldn't embarrass his father, that wouldn't be greeted with even more raucous laughter.

Today, the vendor was making a delivery. The donkey stopped outside of a six-story tenement that housed a café on its first floor. This café was called Hamman al-Nahhasin, *the Coppersmith's Bath*, and a few men were sitting on the fenced-in patio in straw-bottomed chairs, drinking mint or cinnamon tea, eating hardboiled eggs off of copper plates, smoking from the snake-like mouths of water pipes. Samir longed for the leisure of al-Nahhasin. He longed to smoke the sticky ma'assil, the chopped tobacco that was stewed in molasses, fired with red coals, and that made a noise like an underground spring.

But while the vendor attended to his business near the front door, watching his donkey warily, the swarm of boys surrounded Samir and his father. One came up to Samir and put his hand on the donkey's flank.

—Are you a miniature baby donkey shit? Can you see us, little blind boy?

—Ignore them, Samir.

—Leave us alone.— Samir said, his voice rising and asserting itself above the noise of the crowd. And then: —I'm not blind.

The other boy laughed.

—Leave you alone? Why? You're both so much fun. And anyway, you're the lucky one. My father was shot last month in the sting.

The sting. Samir looked at the boy carefully. This meant that the boy's father had been a patriot, a soldier in the war for national independence. The story of the sting was everywhere, and its participants were becoming legendary.

Every night, of course, Cairo was extinguished, a basic wartime precaution. It toppled into darkness, a complete black that was supposed to make the city impregnable to attack from the air. But over the past few months, the German airstrikes had been strangely accurate, and had destroyed government buildings and British barracks, pounding the Allies with a fierce efficiency. Eventually, hoping to unravel the secret of the devastation, British forces organized their own raid. They rang the sirens as usual, making all the normal, and seemingly frantic, preparations. Except instead of Luftwaffe roaring over the city, it was the British navy and its Folgores.

What their pilots saw was a remarkably simple deception. Men had gathered in rings around the British army buildings. They were standing on their own rooftops and smoking cigarettes and, in the completely darkened city, a ring of burning cigarettes looked like a clearly marked bullseye. The smokers were leading the German planes directly toward the most critical British targets. In the morning arrests were made. Most of the conspirators were shot.

Whether or not the boy was telling the truth, Samir felt a visceral, blossoming envy. His father was pathetic in comparison, a pale and stuttering cripple. Why did his father have to be blind? Why couldn't he do something, something truly spectacular, like smoke cigarettes on a rooftop, or fight with the British? Cairo was at war. Why couldn't his father be a patriot, too?

THROUGH THE HAZE OF DIRT and the explosion, Samir dreams of becoming an American citizen. He dreams the cup of the Hollywood Bowl, of marbled aisles and plush velvet chairs, of a sea of gold-stitched tapestries, of a shimmering breath of glamour, oxidized, in the air. Even the pigeons, nested in the scaffolding of Stage Right, seem unusually fluffy. In his dream, Marilyn Monroe administers the oath of citizenship, wearing a tight red dress that pinches and folds her skin. She is ample, she hands him a certificate and kisses him, gently, on the cheek. Her lipstick lingers. They are on stage together, and this, for Samir, is a supremely erotic experience.

And then there are forms, and voices, and Marilyn Monroe dissolves, and there are only soldiers, crowding around him, looming above him. He's lying on a bed of some kind, a single, military-style cot, and he can smell the ether, a potent raw egg smell, and people are talking over him, a doctor perhaps, or a nurse, but the words are incoherent.

And he slips back into his dream, where he has married Marilyn Monroe, and lives on the side of a hill in Southern California, in the kind of house that you see in the newsreels. They have a swimming pool, filled with perfectly clear water, and they keep greyhounds in a pen near the driveway. —Why greyhounds?— Marilyn asks him in Arabic, and he just smiles mysteriously. Actually, he's not sure himself why they have greyhounds, but it's his dream, after all, and he doesn't have to admit anything. He swims, goes and feeds the greyhounds, lays beside the pool to rest, and then someone puts something on his face, and his hand moves instinctively to take it off, and he finds himself holding a frog.

Samir's eyes open. Everything spins, and he's back in the single cot, its blankets sweaty against his skin. Samir sits up.

—Hello! Thought that might work. What's your name, boy?

It's a soldier, one of the soldiers who were watching him juggle at the barracks fence.

—How long asleep?— Samir asks.

—You speak English?

—Of course I speak English.

Samir closes his eyes for a moment. His arms and legs are tingling slightly. They feel almost like they aren't a part of him at all. He truly is surprised that he can speak English. He's never tried, really, not with another living person, and so it's all new to him, a strange vocabulary, bulky as rocks on the tongue. He opens his eyes and looks at the frog. Its skin has faded and dried, it feels like sandpaper in the palm of his hand.

—What...?

He waves weakly to his bed, the infirmary, the other cots.

—Stray artillery shell. Sorry about that. The fences really should be expanded farther into the city.

The soldier lapses into silence. He's looking down at his hands, which are clasped, loose and dangling, at the side of the bed.

Samir looks around at the room. It's exactly like he'd imagined, a military hospital through and through. Scrubbed white walls, two parallel rows of cots, small windows, pillows. An actual sleeping pillow. He has never seen one before, though he has heard of them from his father. The floors are wooden planks, seamed with dirt. Everything, even his bed, has wheels. There are a few other patients, but they seem mostly to be asleep. Only one is visibly wounded, with a voluminous bandage wrapped around his head, a halo of white gauze.

And then there's this soldier. He's an American, and wearing an olive colored uniform. *US Army* is stitched in small, precise letters beneath his collarbone. He looks ashamed, and his already pale face fades to an even more ashen color. *He feels badly,* Samir thinks, and then an unanswered question floats back into his head.

—How long here?— He asks again, and this time there is a note of panic in his voice.

—Ah, listen. Well, the other guys and I, we bought you this. And you know, it should help, I mean, when you get out of here.

And the soldier is holding an odd object, a crutch with wheels attached to it, and suddenly, his whole body prickling with horror, fear gathering in beads along the curve of his back, Samir looks down at his legs. There is a long scar on his left thigh. The scar snakes downward and, lifting the covers, Samir finds that it ends in nothing, in air, in no knee, no shin, no foot, in only absence, and vague pain where the absence is and the pain shouldn't be.

THIS IS THE WAY BONES HEAL, he says to himself later, and the way wounds close, and the way that a jagged bone gradually becomes dull and cased in the skin. Skin grows in a radial arc, it builds under the scabs, an industry of cells. It is the bawáb of the wound, keeping the door to the body shut, trying earnestly to stave off the infection.

—Does he have family?

—No. He's an orphan, I think.

Twenty-one weeks in the infirmary, and then he receives clearance to stay on the base, in the barracks, even after he's healthy. The soldiers have made an appeal, and their commander has agreed, unofficially, to keep the boy on staff. He'll travel with the 7th Infantry Division, newly deployed in the region, and serve as an interpreter and cook. They'll leave before February's rains get too heavy. The resistance in the desert outside of Cairo weakens with every month, the soldiers tell Samir, and there will be nothing to worry about.

Before sunrise, on the morning that he's supposed to leave for the desert, Samir climbs carefully out of his bed. He pulls on his galabiyya—and the thin cloth feels foreign to him now. He limps by the guards with a nod. No one questions him, perhaps because of his missing leg, and he's absorbed by the city again, enmeshed by its sounds and sensations for the first time in so long.

It hurts to walk. The pain nearly knocks him over, and he's unsteady on his crutch-like contraption, a small-wheeled pedestal, really, that's commonly issued to the soldiers who step on mines. The wheels are meant for smooth hospital floors, and on the streets of Cairo they rattle and threaten to break. Samir must move very slowly. He's overwhelmed. In the infirmary, his days were mostly the same. He had forgotten the sounds and scents of the city.

He passes the new stock exchange on Al-Sherifein Street, marveling at the rise of its four Doric columns through the dark. He imagines his mother's joy, his father's delight upon seeing him. His parents will be shocked and sickened, he realizes, by his densely-wrapped leg, but still they will welcome him and celebrate his arrival. Perhaps his mother will slaughter a chicken. Then he will tell them the best news: That he will be traveling with the American army, and perhaps going to America. That he will bring them from Cairo to his new home in Hollywood, as soon as the war is over and he becomes the world's first one-legged major motion picture star.

Samir approaches the tenement building from the alley, and his first impulse is to check the chicken-pen. Only two in there, and they peck immediately at the light, resentful. He closes the lid. Just through the front door, now, and he hears movement in the stairwell above him. *This must be father*, he thinks. And then Samir feels suddenly cold, and a dizziness shoots through him, radiating from his shattered leg. He staggers back into the courtyard and, not thinking about what he's doing, he sprawls behind an old crate, long-since discarded near the wall. Dirt stains the perfect white of his bandages.

From behind the crate he can see the entrance to the building. His parents walk out together, stooped over and fragile. His mother comes first, holding his father's hand. She seems heavier, a heaviness that has settled along her sides, in abutments of fat. Samir's father clings to his mother's hand; even from far away Samir can see how desperately Yusef holds it, his aging fingers clasped and locked into place. Samir's own hand tingles for a moment, as if it is being held.

He wants to leap up and say: *Look, here I am! I'm back, I haven't disappeared! I'm alive!* But something stops him, and he sits there in the dust, watching his mother lead his father towards the edge of the courtyard and the street. Samir hears the regular clatter of hooves. Then he sees the hateful white donkey. It chews stupidly at its lip.

Yusef Habib stands near the donkey, his head down. Fatima

puts its tail in his hand, stroking her husband's hair. And then, with an intimacy that burns at Samir's stomach, she holds her husband's head in her hands. She rests it on her shoulder. She is saying something. They stand there for a moment, the fruit vendor and the French tutor and his wife. *What a strange scene*, Samir thinks, and then: *Is my father crying?* He turns his head away. He can't look; instead he watches the sky, which is just beginning to broaden with the dawn. Then the hooves begin again, and the donkey clatters into the alley, pulling its human freight.

Samir looks back at the courtyard, and sees his mother—who is only a few meters from his hiding place—turn and walk back towards the pen. She reaches down and opens its lid. The chickens make surprised noises, sputtering and clucking softly. *I could say something to her*, Samir thinks, *it would be so easy*. He could just stand up from behind the crate like a ghost. She would be happy to see him, his mother, happy and terrified, and she would go running after his father, yelling that their prayers had been answered, that their son had finally returned.

But the day is cool, and much of Samir's skin is exposed. The cold sweetens along his neck, chills the ball of his spine. He watches his mother stand over the pen and shake her head and sigh. For a long time she stands there and looks down, and still Samir says nothing, immobilized by a pressure that he can't describe to himself or even understand. Finally, Fatima bends down and scoops up the chickens. They struggle wildly in her fists, and she tries to soothe them with her voice. She starts to sing a song, a simple melody that seems familiar to Samir.

Numb, almost anesthetized, he watches his mother put the birds under her arm, like so much luggage, and walk back into the building. The sun is full in the sky.

Nine Songs, or, Who I Am, Where I'm From

Once—wobbling above the Ukraine in an Aeroflot jet—I heard a muffled thump from behind the closed cockpit door. I didn't think anything of it; there was vodka to drink, and there were chickens swirling up and down the aisle of the plane. On Aeroflot, strange noises were part of the routine. They were a welcome relief, in fact, from the sickly, sputtering drone of the engines. But then, one hour later, we landed in Tashkent to a runway crowned with emergency-response vehicles.

—What happened? I asked the flight attendant.

—Oh, nothing, she said. It is just that the pilot is dead.

Smoking cigarettes and drinking in the cockpit, he had suddenly collapsed—his heart stilled—on the instrument panel. Shaken by the impact of his dead body, the controls for the landing gear had ceased functioning. Until the plane actually touched down, the surviving co-pilot was unsure if the wheels were engaged or retracted, if they were active or if they were cradled mutely in the shell of the plane.

twice, on a vacantly raining Saturday morning in November of 1991, my parents and I drove off to Seattle-Tacoma International Airport. At the gate we met Kristina Zale, an eighty-year-old woman whose face my mother only vaguely remembered. She was my great-aunt, and the first relative to emigrate from Latvia since the collapse of the Soviet Union, only months before. She had only one suitcase.

We talked quietly as we walked from baggage claim to the car; we moved from the suburban airport to the gray city; we stopped at the supermarket to buy something for dinner. After a few minutes in the store, we realized that we'd lost Kristina. I rambled up and down the aisles, looking for a frail woman wearing a ragged, hand-knit sweater and polyester slacks.

When I found her in the produce section, I wasn't sure what to do. Her hand was resting on the display of globe-bright tomatoes. She had a basket at her feet, clutched between her calves. It was full, almost overflowing with cucumbers, bananas, lettuce, oranges. She was just standing there, and her hands were moving systematically over the tomatoes on the shelf. She cupped each one in her hand and paused, nodding as if she was counting through her disbelief. The swollen, veined skin beneath her eyes was wet from crying.

YOU RETURN TO THE DOWNTOWN BUS STATION, where you sit in the darkness and imagine poems. The words, bright as the eyes of mice, rise off of the page. You close your eyes and in the black you breathe through your mouth—you try to feel the air, to capture a sense of it with your jaw.

You've traveled far and the weight of your bag has broken a line into your hand. You've traveled with your hands and the weight of distance has broken your bag, has marked you with ink. Your face, where you've slept, reads: Vermont Trailways.

You drink the bus station coffee. You don't worry about

the heartburn. *There's worse things than heartburn*, you figure. Look, though, notice this: The margin of the styrofoam cup is stained and bitten. The coffee will discolor your teeth. It will give musk to your breath, and heat.

Look. It's there—what you're searching for—the driver turns to the small terminal and announces that he's leaving, and his boot catches, briefly, in a space near the doorway, bright and accidental. You get on the bus. Look. It's there, again—the road ribbons from strip malls to strip mines, to the limestone quarries that pop the soil, that surprise the earth and build new, poisoned hills beside the old. Look. It's there—the noisy engine rolls back into the station, the geese scatter in a bright and dirty burst. (Their eyes see only in maps.)

The door to the bus opens and you see the slope of the hill beneath you. The reek of manure comes up from the fields.

You're home.

ONCE, I received a letter from a friend that had no return address. I opened the envelope and the paper leapt out. It was origami smoke, silver and white, and it unfolded itself into language. His signature was illegible—nothing more than a scrawl, a few letters in smoke ink, floating near my collar.

TWICE, HAVE YOU HEARD of Dostoevsky's last dream? You ask, suddenly interjecting your voice into the quiet. Dostoevsky, you continue, was in bed. He'd had a blood clot or a hemorrhage. He was dying. On his second-to-last night, he dreamed of a full moon—rising in the east—that broke into three parts and then came together three times. There was a shield on the moon, and the words, 'yes, yes' were engraved on the shield. Ask everyone, he told his secretary, ask everyone. He never got an answer. He died five days later.

Some friends and I, my cousin says, were walking home from a football match in August of 1991. As we walked down a suburban road just outside of Riga—six or seven of us, I forget—we saw a *Lada* hurtling towards us. It was a little green car, smaller than a horse, and as it came closer and closer, it became clear that the driver meant to run us down. We leapt, all of us as one, off of the road and down a little gravel embankment, into a concrete drainage ditch. The car had missed us, fortunately, but it spun to a stop fifty meters down the road. The engine churned, the gears meshed violently, and the little thing ticked back again.

—What's wrong with you? The driver yelled, his head struggling to pop through the space of his opening window. The Soviet Union's finished. Don't you know that boys your age are dying downtown?

Couldn't you just remind me, couldn't you just whisper it in my ear, like that, like that with your tongue, softly, soft like that, soft like laughter?

In Portbou, Spain, there is a monument to Walter Benjamin,

the writer and theorist who died there in 1940, fleeing from the Nazi takeover of France. Benjamin was a puncture of brilliance and text, an artisan of capturing idea in the brief hollowing of language. Standing near his gravesite—on the high, clean cliff above the Mediterranean—you will see two rusted iron triangles, each twice the size of a person, that jag from the cement of the vine-broken parking lot. Situate yourself within this corroded geometry and look downward. You will see a staircase, forged of the same iron, that leads into the side of the cliff. The sea, roiling and white-topped, is at the bottom of the steps, visible through a glass partition. If you are there in the afternoon, the glass will reflect your outline, give you nothing but a darkened gray shape. Sure, why not—you can walk down the steps. There are eighty-six in total. At the sixty-eighth, you will reach the glass, the scuff of your shoes against the floor ceasing to reverberate. It will be slightly colder at this terminus, and you may shiver as you read the inscription, something about the memory of the nameless.

THIS IS WHAT I REMEMBER: My mother's poor voice, always willing to search for the melody, the Latvian hymns rolling out with an eager awkwardness. And my father's smoke-filled voice, singing French lullabies, or singing in Latin at Mass, precise and accented and yes, beautiful.

Pauls Toutonghi was born in 1976 in Seattle to a mixed Latvian and Egyptian family. His earliest memories involve being confused by a babble of languages. His work has appeared in numerous periodicals, including the *Boston Review*, *Glimmer Train*, *Pittsburgh Quarterly*, and *Book Magazine*. He was the winner of the *Zoetrope: All-Story* First Annual Short Fiction Competition. He has been awarded a Fulbright Grant for study in Latvia in 1999, as well as a 2001 Pushcart Prize. In 2002, Pauls received an honorable mention in the Associated Writing Programs Intro Journals Project. He received his MFA from Cornell University. Pauls lives in upstate New York with his wife, Whitney, and their St. Bernard.